A SHIFTER'S BODYGUARD

PALE MOONLIGHT, BOOK 5

MARIE JOHNSTON

LE PUBLISHING

Being the Synod's resident ballbuster hasn't made Sylva the most popular of her kind, but it's worth the opportunity to lead her people and help those who are like she once was: isolated, powerless, and afraid. But words fail her when her aversion to violence requires a protection detail—a tall, dark, and brooding bodyguard who has no problem fighting with hands, fangs, or claws.

Harrison has spent his adult life protecting his kind—and guarding his broken heart. When he's tasked with keeping Sylva safe from her former pack, the job should be nothing he can't handle. But the closed-off, pacifist female makes him want things he thought he'd lost long ago.

Sylva fights her battles with words, but to stay alive, she needs to take lessons from a shifter who'd rather draw blood than speak. Harrison knows all too well that words can be as sharp as knives, but if he can't convince his charge to trust him, she'll be the one hurt worst of all. They say opposites attract, but in this case, if they can't meet in the middle, it will get them killed.

CHAPTER 1

It was a dark and stormy night...

And something wanted to kill her.

Sylva Raymore peered out the window from behind the curtain in her living room. Something wasn't right. Her bones practically vibrated with the wrongness. She hadn't been filled with this much foreboding since her heinous mating.

The feelings washing over her made her want to run and hide in a closet. Just when she'd thought those days were done

Who'd want to hurt her?

Some days on her job, she could ask who *didn't* want to see her dead. She had enemies. Of course she did. As one of two shifters on the Synod, if she wasn't making enemies, then she wasn't doing her job. Other than nasty emails and deliberate glares when she stopped at the grocery store though, there had never been any major problems.

Tonight, her nerves said that was about to change.

Rain splattered the window. Bursts of lightning lit her

yard and showed nothing but looming evergreens ringing the space.

Still peering into the darkness, she wished for the first time that she'd accepted the apartment at Synod headquarters. It would've even been fully paid for, but after she'd been freed from the confines of her horrible mating, living at the beck and call of anyone, even her own organization, hadn't appealed to her.

Besides, she was pretty damn proud of her home. Furnishing it with what was left of her savings after her mate had met the business end of a silver-laced bullet, she'd made this little cottage into a home. Deep in the forested hills of northern Minnesota, she could shift into her wolf and run in the US or cross into Canada, depending on the path she took. Wolves weren't questioned by border patrol. She had the isolation she'd always craved. No longer would she have to live around shifters she despised, shifters who dictated her every action, or shifters who didn't give two rabbit turds about her welfare. She was her own female.

And she happened to rule those shifters now. So, bonus.

You are a leader. If she told herself that enough, would it keep her from running and hiding? *Strong shifters do not hide in closets. Strong shifters take care of themselves. Strong shifters can think their way through a situation without resorting to bloodshed.*

She repeated her mantra as she searched the night for what had caused the warning tingles plaguing her.

Was that movement in the trees behind her garden? She narrowed her eyes, calling on the innate keen eyesight of her kind. Her gardens—her pride and joy—were on the other side of the garage to her left. She couldn't view them, but the trees beyond them were visible whenever lightning lit the sky.

Thunder rattled the house. Was it just the storm that had her out of sorts?

No, she'd weathered a hundred storms since she'd lived here. It was never thunder that had terrified her, but her mate's thundering voice.

She concentrated on the area again. Whatever it was had quit moving, but she wouldn't waste a dollar betting that it was nothing more than a deer. The instinct to curl into a ball swelled until she could choke on it. No. She wasn't that female who cowered in the corner once the scent of danger rose. Not anymore.

She backed away from the window and dropped to her hands and knees. Crawling across the floor, she made it to the narrow window by her entry door. All the lights were off, and she'd even turned off the TV to make it look like she'd gone to bed for the night. Inching upward to look outside, she scanned her yard, searching for movement.

She was a lone wolf, literally, but being by herself right now really sucked.

Maybe she should dig out that old pistol. It had been the one item she'd taken from her previous home that wasn't hers. Everything she'd owned had fit into a simple two-by-two box with room to spare. Roman had controlled every nuance of her life. And she hadn't taken that damn gun because she'd wanted it, but she couldn't bring herself to get rid of it either.

The last thing she wanted to do was touch that six-shooter, but as the hairs of her arms quivered, she either needed to shift into her wolf or arm herself—or hide.

Strong shifters do not hide in closets. Strong shifters take care of themselves. Strong shifters can think their way through a situation without resorting to bloodshed.

The last part of her affirmation rang false at the moment.

Danger vibrated the air around her. Maybe she shouldn't have skipped all the self-defense courses offered by the Guardians who served the Synod.

She respected the Guardians, the law enforcement of her kind. The ones who served and protected the Synod were considered part of her pack, but that didn't mean she socialized with them. It didn't mean she did anything but pass on a cool greeting or issue an order.

Buried in the hills and close to the border, they were isolated from civilization, where shifters who far outlived a human's lifetime didn't have to be so vigilant about valid identification. The number of Guardians in her pack was small, but growing, now that the shifter government had combined itself with the vampires' leadership. The Guardians were on good terms with the four other Synod leaders she served with. They were on fair terms with her. She just never asked about family, shared her lack of a social life, or chitchatted in any way.

As for the self-defense courses, she hated for anyone to witness how weak she was. If she had to resort to violence to get her way, then she was no better than her mate. Then there was the matter of the instructors: the womanizing twins who stripped women down to their panties left and right when they grinned. Well, when one twin grinned. The other was brooding and fierce, and when he looked at her, she felt as if he'd stripped her down to her terrified soul.

The two Guardians were perpetually on loan from their home pack because of their connections to the former government and their local roots. They weren't going anywhere anytime soon.

So, no. No self-defense courses.

But she didn't want to use the gun, or even look at it. The memories it'd bring back were too awful to deal with on a night like tonight. She'd shift.

Roman had never allowed her to shift when he was angry with her.

Lowering back down, she slipped her shirt off, unhooked her bra, and dropped it on the floor, then rolled her pants and underwear down. Focusing inward, she shifted. Her senses blazed to life. Smells sharpened with a thousand more facets than in her human form. Her sight in the dark house was as good as if her bedside lamp were on. She wasn't a hunter. She would wait for whatever was out there to come to her.

There. An unusual scent. Her nose twitched. Another shifter.

Something about the scent pricked her memory and not in a good way. Backing into the corner of the entryway, she waited. This was not cowering in a closet. This was lying in wait and it was all the strategy she had. The shifter would smell her wolf, but it wasn't like he'd be scared away.

Who the hell was it? Anyone here on business would have marched up to her porch and knocked. She had no shifter or human neighbors within miles, and during her time living here, no one had ever stopped by. If they did, it wouldn't be during a storm.

The scent grew strong. A male. And familiar.

Her heart hammered as her gaze darted from the door to the windows and around her living room in case the asshole snuck in. She spotted her phone.

Damn.

Calling for help before she'd shifted would've been smart. *Strong shifters can think their way through a situation without resorting to bloodshed.* Her first major chance to prove to herself that she wasn't ridiculous for adhering to her nonviolent ways and she'd shifted. But then if she'd called someone, she'd have others in her business and she'd lived most of her life that way. Never again.

The scent rolled in like a wall of fog. It was so strong, he had to be on her porch. And he was being silent. Not a good sign for her.

His smell snaked through all the invisible cracks and crevices, chasing away the barriers she had erected to keep her past from haunting her. Her nerves erupted until she trembled.

The male smelled like her mate—the one she'd helped kill. The one who had three brothers she'd run from in the middle of a cold, moonless night because turning herself in to the Synod had been better than the punishment the Raymores would dole out. Those days were long behind her and she'd ignorantly and stupidly thought that her position made her untouchable. And she'd made herself accessible by living in the boondocks with neighbors that were miles away.

Faint scuffling sounded outside the front door. "I can smell you, whore."

She jerked back, her ass hitting the wall. Which brother was that? Rafe, John Todd, or Clayton? Their voices were all deep and gruff. The brothers had been so much alike she'd been keenly uncomfortable around them.

Don't panic. Don't panic. Her body wasn't listening, but being in her wolf form helped. Her shift had turned out to be necessary. Her mate's brothers didn't rely on thinking, preferring force to get their way.

She focused on the wood grains of her door. Whichever brother it was, he hadn't shifted yet. He was probably naked so he could shift—or violate her. Consent wasn't a big deal to the Raymore brothers, not with the ferocious status of their entire pack. Neither was monogamy, equality, or legality. None of it mattered to them. They were not only the leading pack of their clan, but their clan was in charge of the colony she'd been born and raised in. A

Raymore's word was law and to hell with what their government said.

She *was* the government now. He couldn't stride up to her porch and terrorize her. She bared her teeth even though no one could see.

"Whore? You know yer gonna get what's coming." His sneer was too close. The door wasn't thick enough. It could be a foot thick and it wouldn't be enough. "Killing my brother. You shoulda turned that gun on yourself."

As if she hadn't debated for hours who she'd use the gun on—Roman or herself. If it hadn't been for her mother... She scratched the thought from her mind. It was safer if everyone thought the deed had been hers, and hers alone.

Alone didn't seem like such a great plan at the moment.

She glanced at her phone again. Why had she shifted? She could've been shooting messages all over the Synod about the danger she was in and who was responsible. A few minutes ago, the thought had been abhorrent, but now it sounded better than facing an enraged male with a reasonable grudge.

That decision had been made. She had to move forward. She only scented one brother. If either of his other brothers was around, she was screwed. But she'd survived Roman. She could survive this.

Roman and his brothers were alike. They ruled by entitlement and brute force. All she had to do was create an opening to call for help. Her mind rebelled at the thought. Just one person. That was all who'd know.

But who could she call? The list was short. There was the other shifter serving on the Synod with her, Demke. He was always inviting her out to his place with his mate and kids. She'd never taken him up on the offer but she was friendlier with him than with the other three Synod members. Demke would be discreet.

"Whore. I can smell your fear."

Whore. That one word stoked the rebellious side that she rarely expressed. That one word described how the Raymores treated females that weren't their own kin.

Hearing it again emboldened her to change back into her human form. "I'm surprised you were the one to find me first. You were always the stupidest of the litter."

A snarl cut through the night. The brothers all looked alike, and they resented being referred to as a litter. There were ten months between each one, their mother being resigned to the same fate that Sylva had once been locked into. How had their grandma amassed all her power? Was she still the matriarch?

Did it matter? The Raymore on her doorstep was the one she needed to worry about.

Vulnerability hung heavy around her shoulders. She was naked and unarmed. Unlike most shifters, she was self-conscious about her nudity. If she lunged for her phone, he'd see her in the window. Should she run and grab a knife from the kitchen? Her stomach twisted at the thought of sinking a blade into flesh.

He was still in his human form. Maybe she should shift back to her wolf. She didn't want to fight, but letting him ravage her wasn't an option.

Before she could make her decision, he was speaking, his sinister tone breaking through the downpour. "Did you think your new job would protect you? I'll never forget what you did to my baby brother."

Or would he never forget that he hadn't had the chance to do to her what Roman had? Because Roman had threatened to offer her up to his brothers, and it had only been a matter of time.

"I dream about killing Roman every night." She laughed

loud enough for him to hear, but her stomach churned. Would he smell her lie? She gambled that what she said would make him angry and predictable. "It's the next best thing to actually doing it, and I wish I could put him in the crosshairs over and over again."

The door shook and she jumped back, her body slamming into the wall. Mission accomplished. He was furious. She shifted and settled her weight on her haunches. When that door broke free of its hinges, she'd run or pounce. All she had to do was get away, and she'd done it once already.

Her anxiety calmed only slightly in wolf form. She was a shifter and counted on the innate self-defense instincts she'd been born with—since that was her only option.

"You bitch!" The door rocked and wood splintered. Her heart rammed into her throat and it was like Roman rose from the dead just to sneer in her ear. *You think you can take him? A weak, little thing like you against a Raymore? He'll eat you for lunch and lick you clean for dessert.*

The heavy wood of her front door broke free of the latch. There was nowhere to run in her house and he'd blocked her path to freedom—if she could even outrun him. That left her with one option if she wanted to survive whatever he planned.

When he wedged his body through an opening large enough to get through, she leapt. He wasn't ready for her, nor was he expecting her to make the first move.

He instinctively put his arms up, but her momentum crushed them between their bodies as they toppled backward. She locked her jaws around his neck and dug her claws into his shoulders. Grinding her teeth together with all the force she could summon, she dug for his carotid. This close and with the taste of him flooding her mouth, she could finally identify him. John Todd. Bleeding him out was her best chance at weakening him. His startled yell turned to a gurgle, but the surprise of her attack didn't last long enough.

A punch landed on her side. She whimpered but didn't let go. Another punch. Blinding pain, but she maintained her hold. It became a game of who would collapse first. He'd have to break a few more ribs to get her to quit. Thanks to his brother, she had no problem weathering a few broken bones.

He bucked underneath her, but she rabbit kicked him with her hind legs, hitting all the soft spots she could find. He heaved and wailed his fists against her sides, but each blow landed with less strength than the previous one.

She inhaled fire with each breath but refused to let go. She wouldn't be the first one to quit. Warm blood oozed between her lips and over her muzzle. John Todd jerked underneath her and finally went still. She hung on even longer, working her jaws back and forth for maximum impact.

Fatigue weighed on her. What was she doing? He wasn't fighting her anymore. He wasn't moving, but his heart still beat. A crack of thunder startled her and she released. Staggering off him, she slipped and slid on the porch. Whether it was slick from blood or rain, she didn't know.

When her teeth had been buried in his neck, she'd been ready to kill him. Many would say she *should* have killed him, but the thought made her gag on the metallic taste in her mouth. There was another way of dealing with him. There had to be. The Raymores were all about to get their way, she couldn't be just like them.

And yet, he'd heal eventually, and he wouldn't quit coming for her. His other brothers might not have cared to show, but they would come as a pack when they learned how she'd hurt him.

Fear hammered at her mind. They'd come for her. Just like Roman stomping through the house, the strikes of his boots marring the floor, they'd tear through her house and destroy all she'd worked for.

A strangled noise came from her. She couldn't take them all. She couldn't deal with this unconscious male. Nor could she move and finish her kill by chewing his head off.

Her old self took over. *Run.*

She swung her head toward the dark woods. Woods so much like that night. Were the others out there? Were they waiting to corner her?

Her mind spun over her options and stuck on how badly she wanted to call for help. Shifting as she charged inside, she tripped as she raced toward her phone. Somehow she managed to dial Demke. She was on autopilot.

When he answered, she gasped, "I've been attacked."

Alarmed, but calm, he asked, "Are you at your house?"

"Yes, and I don't know if there are more coming."

"Get to a safe place. I'm sending help."

Help. She had help.

Everyone will know you're weak. Everyone will find out what happened with Roman. Everyone will know that you didn't have the guts to finish off John Todd. Everyone will know that you're a fake, that you're just scared. Always scared.

She gulped in air and tossed her phone away. Shivering like she was lost in a snowstorm, she hesitated. She didn't want to be that female again, but she was. The more her body shook, the more she relied on previous experience.

Hide. Get to a safe place.

Pushing her hair out of her face with a shaky hand, she glanced around. A dark place. A place where *he* wouldn't find her. But he always found her. Closets, bathrooms, stairwells, he always found her.

Her cellar. Her precious cellar, where she'd be surrounded by her passion. Racing downstairs on rubbery legs, she kept expecting to hear heavy footsteps from behind her. A peal of thunder and she missed two steps, catching herself on the railing.

Once her feet hit the carpet of her basement, she went straight for the cellar. It didn't have a lock. *Shit.* It didn't have a lock and John Todd wasn't dead.

The pistol. Her eyes filled with tears. No. No. Her gaze strayed to the stairs. Damn! She darted to the spare bedroom next door and headed straight for the closet that held the little rectangular box she'd wanted to forget existed but couldn't live without.

Flipping the lid off, she closed her bloody hand around the cold handle. It was shaking. Holding the gun away from her, she rushed back to her cellar and closed the door. Complete darkness descended. Sinking onto her ass in the farthest corner, she half-heartedly pointed the gun in the direction of the door and tried not to vomit the taste of John Todd out of her mouth.

And she waited.

His damn phone kept going off. Harrison Wallace glared at the shiny surface of the bar counter. His twin Malcolm was in the dark corner opposite the pool table, making out with a hot blond who had legs for miles. The shifter female must've agreed to be with both of them, otherwise Malcolm would've moved on to a new target.

Needing his brother to pick up their fun for the night should dent his ego but it didn't. Harrison knew he wasn't much fun to be around, just like he knew that a female would only be with him because Malcolm had charmed the pants off her first.

It might be easier if it had been fun in the beginning. Had he ever had fun? Sex felt good, there was no doubt about that, but he was starting to miss a connection, a meaning that was about more than getting off. He knew better than anyone that there'd never be a connection for him.

A mate was no longer written in the stars for him.

All these years later, his lack of a mate was becoming more noticeable as several of his fellow Guardians settled down with their mates to be sickeningly happy. Their pack was hours south, in West Creek. The West Creek Guardians. But he and Malcolm had offered to drive up and help the Synod's Guardians with the government's transition—which, to be honest, was as transitioned as it'd get—and then they'd never left. But the few Guardians who worked for the Synod were blissfully young, and if fate didn't hate him, they wouldn't find their mates and get all sloppy eyed for many years yet.

He wanted the same for Malcolm, but his mating ship had sailed, too. Still, could Malcolm find someone one day? It was possible to mate without being destined to be together. But it wouldn't happen with Harrison's morose ass weighing Malcolm down.

He should go over there. He should *want* to go over to Malcolm and the blond and get the night started. But look at that, his phone was ringing.

Suddenly grateful for the interruption, he looked at the screen. What the hell was Demke calling him for? He and Malcolm sometimes did more than odd jobs for the Synod's members, but they were rarely called when they were off-duty.

Before joining the West Creek pack, he and Malcolm had grown up only a half hour away. Tame Peaks was a small colony, but it was the closest one to the Synod and essentially a "government town," as the humans would say. Once upon a time, their father had been part of the shifter government. The *former* shifter government.

Those who whined for the good old days didn't complain as much when the sons of a former Lycan Council member arrived on their doorstep on behalf of the Synod and ordered them to change their ways. Especially since their father was wasting away in jail.

Wasting away. Harrison snorted as he picked the phone up off the bar top. Father was biding his time in prison like it was a five-star hotel. The twins had their dad's blessing to help the Synod, and it was nice to work close to home, even if they weren't a close family. The Synod benefited because the people viewed the twins as a bridge between the old government and the new.

Only one ring left before it'd go to his automated voicemail. Harrison answered but he hadn't even said hello when Demke's voice cut in. "Get to Sylva's. She's in trouble. One attacker for sure. She doesn't know how many others."

"Got it." Harrison flicked his phone off as he pivoted off the barstool. Sylva. In trouble. "We gotta go," he called in Malcolm's direction as he headed for the door.

Malcolm wrenched his lips off the blond and frowned over his shoulder. All it took was one glance at Harrison's face to know how serious the situation was. Without a word to the female, he pushed away. She shrugged and grabbed a pool cue. She'd have no trouble finding another partner.

"What's going on?" his brother asked as they rushed out of the bar. The rain had let up and the storm was passing.

"Demke called. Sylva's been attacked and she's still in trouble."

His twin jerked his head over to peer at him. "And he called *us*? Sylva hates us."

He nodded as they both climbed into Malcolm's navy-blue, four-door pickup. Technically, the truck was both of theirs, but he was content to let Malcolm take the lead in most everything. Besides, they did everything together—eating, fighting, fucking. Everything.

Nights like tonight, Harrison wished he were more like his brother. Malcolm could have a relationship with anyone he wanted; he didn't have to share. But neither one had met anyone special, someone who made them feel as if things could be…different.

Malcolm kept talking as he stomped on the gas. They fishtailed out of the parking lot. "I mean, hell, of course we'll help her. But I feel like we're gonna scare her worse, charging onto her property." Malcolm rubbed a hand over his beard as he maneuvered through town toward the highway that would take them to Sylva's. They'd never been out there, but part of their job was protection, and knowing where all the Synod members lived was their duty.

"Demke must have known we'd be in town." They had a reputation. When they were off duty, they were off duty. Their lively personal lives seemed to be the talk of Synod headquarters.

Harrison had never understood it. It wasn't like it was a hobby that they were good at. It was just sex. A lot of it, granted, but they were shifters. Unmated shifters. Shifters who had each lost their chance with a fated mate, though no one else knew that. Well, their parents knew, but Father wasn't talking about anything more than Final Four scores, and Maw wanted everyone to leave her the hell alone.

"You think she's scared of us?" Harrison didn't care for Sylva and her high-and-mighty attitude, but the last thing he wanted to do was scare her.

Malcolm waved his hand. "She hides it well, but yeah,

probably. Don't get me wrong, she doesn't like us either. But I think it stems from fear and not true hate."

That would explain why she never came to their self-defense and marksmanship courses. Of all the shifters who should've attended, she was at the top of the list. But it didn't matter how many times he or Malcolm bugged the rest of the Synod leaders about it, she didn't show. Maybe she knew how to defend herself. Or maybe she really fucking hated them.

"Has Dr. Phil called to request your unique insight on the female mind?" Harrison didn't mean to be flippant. How had his twin been able to deduce that much about her when to him she was nothing but a petite cloud of mystery? Mystery and vexation. The way she looked at him, it was the way people had viewed him his whole life: the less desirable brother.

"No, but I sent him a message that I'm around whenever he needs me."

Leave it to Malcolm to remain unruffled. Harrison reached into the backseat of the pickup and dug out their weapons. When he turned back around in his seat, he had their duffel bag full of goodies.

He handed a shoulder holster to his twin. Malcolm shrugged into it without swerving off the road. Harrison stashed his own knives in the tops of his boots and slipped on another shoulder holster. Like Malcolm's, it held both a blade and a gun.

Malcolm pushed their speed a few notches faster than was safe, but the wet roads still held him back. His brother shouldn't let that slow him. Harrison's urge to get to Sylva's side was inexplicable, other than that he'd never failed a mission. Only once, but since then, never.

As he stared out the windshield, trees flew past the pickup. A cloud of dust whipped up behind them, but that didn't stop his twin from lowering the window an inch. He didn't have to ask why. There might be more shifters around and they might not be friendly. Any scent he and his twin could detect would help them determine who or what was after her or if there were more attackers lying in wait.

He didn't pick up on anything unusual. Pine, birds that were native to the area, and maybe a bear or two, but they gave shifters a wide berth.

"ETA two minutes," Malcolm said. That matched Harrison's own estimate.

A smell hit him. Male and sour, like milk that had been left out in the sun too long.

"Don't know that one," Malcolm murmured.

The threat against Sylva wasn't coming from anyone they had ever been in contact with. The shifter could've been hired out, or maybe it was a personal attack. He recalled the first time he'd seen her in her prison cell. So small. Curled in on herself. Distrustful of everyone and everything. He'd heard her story and couldn't believe that she had killed her abusive mate.

She'd blossomed once she was appointed to the Synod. Strong and outspoken, she was untouchable and the biggest supporter of shifter rights, fighting to insert the Synod's presence into the most isolated colonies. With her, the Synod had a conscience that advocated for compromise and nonviolent solutions. Sometimes, she took her role too far, as if she wanted to make violence obsolete.

Did she subconsciously hold his role in freeing her against him? He'd seen her at her weakest and she couldn't, or wouldn't, forget it. The way she couldn't seem to tolerate being in the same room as him or his brother, combined with her uncompromising leadership, was Sylva 2.0.

He'd seen her unravel some of the strongest males with nothing but words. Then she'd turned around and placed a

Band-Aid on a young's skinned knee. She'd almost smiled. And Harrison had waited breathlessly for it to happen.

Then her gaze had flicked up at him and her typical hardness had returned.

Her little cottage came into view. "Cute" was not a word he'd have ever associated with Sylva. Strong, stolid, businesslike. Those words and all their synonyms related to her. Her appearance was sleek, sophisticated, but not cute like her house.

Malcolm skidded the pickup to a stop between the house and the garage. There was no point in parking farther back and sneaking up on the house. Sylva had already sent out an SOS.

His twin killed the engine and they each got out. They could strip down and shift but he had a feeling he'd need his hands more than his claws.

The smell of rain and blood smacked him in the face. On the porch a dark form twitched. The shifter he had smelled. He exchanged a glance with Malcolm and flowed up the covered porch, taking each of the three stairs slowly.

Malcolm swept around the back. His brother would look for any more threats and search for Sylva outside. Harrison would neutralize this piece of shit on the porch and search inside. He couldn't smell another shifter in the vicinity, except for Sylva. Fear. So much fear.

He checked over the male. The guy wasn't going anywhere with this throat half ripped out. The porch was wet from rain, but dark with blood. Good. Harrison didn't care what this guy's reason for being on Sylva's porch was, he'd gotten what he deserved. The healing would take hours, but as much as Harrison wanted to finish the job and slice the rest of the head away from the body, it would be better to let the shifter heal and question him later. And he still had to find Sylva.

Stepping into the house, her scent swamped him. It was different than when she was at headquarters, softer, more… feminine. Even in the dark he could tell the place was cozy, comfortable. Homey. Definitely not what he'd expected.

He wiped off his boots before starting his search. As he swept through the ground floor, making as little sound as possible, he tried to reconcile this tidy little home with the stern female he knew. It was like two different people.

She wasn't on the ground floor. Her fear was the strongest by the entryway. He went back to the front door and eyed the stairs going down. She would've sought a place where she could defend herself, or at the very least feel safer. As he descended, he knew he was on the right track. Her terror clogged the basement. This wasn't an area she normally spent much of her time in. Her cozy scent wasn't as strong, and there wasn't as much care taken with the decorating. The basement was more like the Sylva he knew. Unadorned and functional.

At the base of the stairs, he tuned in to all of his senses. He couldn't hear whimpering or crying; he could only smell her. She was down here, but where?

There was one closed door in the entire space and fear congealed around it like the blood outside.

He was in the middle of stretching his hand out to grasp the knob when he paused. Sylva had just ripped out the throat of her assailant. It wasn't a good idea to go barging into her safe room.

Dropping his hand, he cleared his throat. "Sylva, it's me. Harrison." He winced. That might make her want to stay in the room.

A moment of silence went by. Could she hear him? He was trying to figure out what to do when a faint noise reached his ears. A whimper? Which form was she in?

"Sylva?" The need to get to her pounded at him, but he kept his tone light and steady. "Can I come in?"

A choking sound and a sniffle, but no response. Was he making progress?

Fuck, this wasn't what he normally dealt with. He was the muscle, Malcolm was the smile. He should've let his twin take the inside. Even as that thought passed through his mind, he wanted to snarl at it.

Gentle. Be soothing. She scares easy. How easy the change came back to him. "Sylva. I'm going to open the door. I'll do it real slow, and if you want me to stop, just say so."

He hadn't heard himself talk like that in… He knew exactly how long. Since before he'd demanded Gloria stay the fuck out of his head so he could concentrate. He squeezed his eyes shut. He hadn't needed to be close to her to know how much he'd hurt her.

Shoving those thoughts away, he inched the door open. "It's me, Harrison," he repeated. A range of smells assaulted him, from tangy to metallic, but it was hers that stood out. So scared. And shame was unmistakable. "I'm going to step inside and I'll have my hands where you can see them." He was talking low, like he would around a baby he didn't want to wake up.

A shaky inhale. "H-Harrison." Good. He wasn't facing a terrified wolf.

"Yes." He didn't advance, but waited, his intuition telling him that if he moved too fast he'd lose all the ground he'd made.

Blood was smeared across her face and down her slender neck. It was the first time he'd ever seen her anything less than put together. Silky black strands were stuck in the dried blood along her cheeks and plastered to her forehead. Her arms were hugged around her knees and she was nude. In her hands was an old six-shooter—pointed at him.

He still didn't move. "Can you put the gun down?" A gut shot wouldn't help the night.

"I hate this gun."

He made the connection without asking more questions. She'd shot her mate and she'd kept the gun. The former Lycan Council might've been corrupt, but they would've held on to the gun with the rest of her belongings. When they'd been overthrown and she'd been released, she must have gotten it back.

"Want me to take it?" he offered.

She lifted her gaze from his knees to his eyes. No, this wasn't the same Sylva that ruled shifters and vampires alike. This was the Sylva from the prison cell. He'd been there, when the Lycan Council had been dismantled. He'd helped free their prisoners. It was where he'd first seen Sylva and learned of her story, imprisoned for shooting silver into her mate. She'd been timid, but defiant, speaking out against the Lycan Council and how they'd failed their people.

But no, this was the Sylva from *before* the prison cell.

Holding her gaze, he lowered to a squat and held a hand out. She didn't fight him, but she didn't aid his effort as he lifted the pistol from her grip. Instead of heaving a sigh of relief or standing up, she hugged herself tighter. He set the pistol on a shelf to his right, next to jars of food. Rows of pickled vegetables lined the shelves. That explained the tangy scent.

He looked back at her. Naked and defenseless. "Do you want my shirt?"

Startled, she dropped her gaze to his black T-shirt. "Y-yes."

He shrugged out of his shoulder holster and lifted his shirt over his head. After handing it to her, he turned around.

The level of fear diminished as she rose and put his shirt on. "You can turn around."

Her voice had regained strength. She was transforming before his eyes. The scared-spitless female was being replaced by the Synod leader. For a second, she looked like an avenging angel. But the fear in her eyes and the obvious effort to keep herself calm dulled the effect.

She feathered her fingers over her forehead and grimaced when her hair pulled and tugged against the dried blood. "Is he…?"

"No. Malcolm's out there watching him." He didn't have to talk to his twin to know. They'd worked together too long for that kind of communication to be necessary anymore. "Do you know who he is?"

Her eyes misted over and she nodded. He waited, but she didn't elaborate.

"Do you think there are others?"

"I'm sure of it." She pulled at the hem of his shirt. It swamped her, but he refused to leer at her bare legs at a time like this. He didn't drop his gaze below her violet eyes.

She continued to fiddle with the hem of the shirt while looking at the pistol. He'd never seen that expression. It never mattered what sort of person stood in front of the Synod—an unbathed male with little more than two quarters to rub together, starving children stricken with body lice, or uninhibited females who smelled like both a brewery and a brothel. Sylva never shied away from them. But from her expression, she'd rather jump off the nearest bridge than touch the gun's metal.

She jerked her hands from the shirt and forced them to her sides. "I'll go get changed. I need to meet with the rest of the Synod." She walked out without looking back.

That was it. He hadn't been expecting profuse thanks, but something more than a dismissal. He gave his head a little shake and followed her. Upstairs, Malcolm's voice drifted in from where he stood over the body on the porch. His brother was on the phone.

Harrison moved to the window by the door and rested one shoulder against the wall, crossing his arms. Hopefully, Sylva knew that she wasn't going to the Synod alone. He didn't put in the energy to argue with anyone, and that extended to her—for tonight. And for tonight, he didn't want to play the bad guy when she only wanted to be left alone.

The minutes ticked by. Malcolm tapped on the window and lifted his chin toward the pickup. It was the only communication he needed. They'd be leaving in the same vehicle whenever Sylva was ready. As twins, they didn't have to talk or, thankfully, mind-speak. He and Malcolm could communicate more in a look than most siblings could say in an hour.

A soft rustle moving through the house caught his attention. Sylva was stepping into some sensible black flats. She was dressed in a black turtleneck that was much too warm for the middle of July and black slacks. Her midnight hair had much of the blood brushed out and was twisted into a bun. The ensemble made her look like a stern ballet teacher, but the outfit was more her style of defense than that pistol.

Her gaze swept the little cottage, touching on everything but him. She folded her hands together in front of her and finally settled her cool gaze on him. "Do you mind taking care of…of *him*…while I meet with the Synod?"

"We're all driving together. You aren't going anywhere alone."

Displeasure rippled through her expression, but there was something else there. She was still scared. "I don't want to drive in the same vehicle as him."

"Who is he?"

"I will wait and discuss the situation with the others." She was back to no-nonsense. Her voice was steady, but her eyes were haunted.

She was scared—and ashamed. "Both Malcolm and I will be with you. You can sit in front, and I'll sit in back. The male will be loaded into the pickup's box. That way you'll have one of us in between you and the attacker at all times."

Her gaze softened as the rest of her stiffened with resolve. "Right. Let's go do this."

CHAPTER 2

Sylva and three of the Synod members were waiting on Demetrius to flash here. As a vampire, he had that ability. Bastian, the other vampire member, had made it here first, but punctuality concerned him more than it did Demetrius. Her fellow shifter Demke was quiet next to her, as if he sensed she would only explain herself once. Demke had been on the Lycan Council, the one member who hadn't used it for his own benefit, the lone shifter who'd cared about bettering his people's future. Jonathon, the Synod's vampire/shifter hybrid and their party of five's unofficial leader, had stumbled in a few minutes ago, no doubt having been called from his mate's warm bed.

Waiting like this allowed her adrenaline to wind down and her dread at explaining the situation to pile up. Headquarters was quiet. Only a few Guardians discreetly roamed the manicured acres surrounding the long, rectangular building.

One end housed the prison, the apartments, and the spattering of departments that served the Synod's needs: financial offices, Guardian offices, and a small medic office for any major injuries that could use a hand in healing. The one-story portion where the Synod met and conducted business had been dark when they pulled up.

How much longer? The chamber was quiet. There'd be no speakers tonight, just her, and she'd do it sitting in her chair at the table on the dais others normally stood before.

Why had she put on the turtleneck? It was hot and clingy. Add in how she usually felt when Harrison was around and she was really freaking uncomfortable. She couldn't stand the helpless way her body flushed when he was nearby.

Yet when she'd heard his voice on the other side of the cellar door, she'd wanted nothing more than to fling herself into his arms and let him shelter her from the rest of the world.

Following through would've been humiliating. First, she'd had to call for help. And second, she was the beaten-down female who had risen to the most powerful position of her kind. She felt weak around him. Another reason she was annoyed at herself for feeling hot and clingy when he was around.

Harrison was waiting outside the chamber in the receiving area with Malcolm. He'd seen her in a state she'd sworn she'd never let herself be in again. Vulnerable, frightened, and hiding. She despised herself for her reaction. It didn't matter if John Todd was secure in the prison cell she'd once spent months in. But at least dwelling on that irony took her mind off Harrison more than anything else could.

A few years ago, she'd been imprisoned for killing her mate. His family had thought she would burn for it—they would've killed her if they could've caught her—but instead she'd risen to rule her people. Now she was all too happy to let that family waste away up there, wondering if anyone in the world was ever going to support them. Except John Todd had two more brothers, and she had no doubt they were coming for her.

Demetrius entered on a swirl of dewy night air. He closed the chamber doors and rushed to the table. "Apologies."

Sylva couldn't summon her standard dour attitude toward the male. He was charming, like Malcolm, and he seemed to be sincerely sorry that he'd held up the proceedings.

When he was settled, she began recounting her night. "As you know, I was once convicted of killing my mate. He was an insecure, abusive ass. As are his three brothers, one of whom is now in our prison."

Once she'd described the attack, Demke asked, "Why now? You've been on the Synod since the beginning."

"I would guess that the policies I champion are hitting too close to home, threatening their family's totalitarian rule." The Raymores were a perfect example of why their old government had sucked. Packs who ruled their colonies like that should be squashed. "Also, their grandma was ancient when I left. Perhaps she's getting weaker."

"And others might take advantage of the change in power to inform us of their living conditions." Jonathon spoke with the confidence that it'd been confirmed already.

By now, Sylva didn't have to explain. They'd dealt with enough colonies that had tried to ignore the Synod's existence and keep their politics to themselves. A change in leadership could be brutal if the pack heir wasn't liked or respected or strong enough to hold on to the position.

Some packs created conditions to keep their choice in place, packs like her former mate's, the deep-in-the-woods Four Claws. One of those choices was to be situated across the border. The extra effort to drive that far north and get past border security kept the colony isolated.

There were more out there like her old colony and more

shifters like her, males and females shackled by old ideals and victims of the seclusion that shifters often sought for themselves. Her purpose in life had become gathering the power necessary to change the circumstances for those shifters, not to dissolve as soon as she was faced with a big, scary male.

She'd faced John Todd and she was still standing. He'd been injured badly and the reward for defending herself would be two more like John Todd coming after her. She was in grave danger despite being surrounded by the Synod's Guardians. Trepidation made her jittery. Desperation, anxiety, and sheer terror dogged her until it was all she could do to keep her hands from trembling. She clasped them together in front of her and adopted a cool, refined expression.

"What are the other brothers' names?" Jonathan asked.

"Rafe and Clayton Raymore." So close they could be twins, but unlike the twins outside, when Rafe and Clayton had been around, they'd looked at her like she was a chew toy purchased just for their pleasure.

Jonathon scratched notes on a little notepad. "We'll send names and descriptions to the Guardians on duty. If they step foot in town, we'll know."

They wouldn't. The brothers were bold, having lived a life of entitlement, but they weren't stupid.

Demke spoke next. "I'm sure you all know my opinion about what we should do about the Raymore in our prison."

Demetrius frowned, the look doing nothing to detract from his handsome features. "Attacking one of the Synod is a grievous offense. I have no problem executing him."

She hated the urge sweeping through her to concur. She was not like other Raymores. Being mated into the family hadn't made her like them, and she couldn't escape the feeling that killing John Todd while he was imprisoned would nudge her closer to them.

"The *people* might have a problem with us executing him," Bastian replied. "Though I heartily agree he deserves it."

Sylva lifted her chin. "I want him to rot in there at least as long as I did." Poetic justice. More her style.

"Then he can be our guest for as long as needed." Demetrius regarded her, concern heavy in his green eyes. "The brothers are our first priority. Rather, Sylva's safety is our first priority, so we need to deal with the brothers. Tell us everything about them."

Sylva took a measured breath and thought back to that period of her life she never let her mind delve into anymore. "The whole family lived in the colony when I lived there and I doubt that's changed. The brothers were always close, getting away with murder and I'm not exaggerating. I knew… I knew when I did what I did that the wrath of the three of them would bear down on me as one, which is why I fled."

Going to prison had been a relief, in a way. At the time, it'd been the only way to save her mother's life and to keep herself safe. Sylva's disappearance and incarceration had caused enough of a flurry to keep the blame fully on her and protect Mother from being used against her. It'd been part of the plan, the one she'd convinced Mother was best when they were staring down at her dead mate.

The Lycan Council at the time had been a lot of things, but letting three bullheaded shifters get to her wasn't something they would do. It'd look bad for the prison guards and for the council members.

She'd been safe in prison, which had been almost worth the misery of being left alone with nothing to do but remember. "They might try to get John Todd out before they come after me."

Demetrius shrugged. "Why don't we cut them off at the pass and dangle you in front of them like a ripe little bunny?"

There was no way Demetrius knew her family nickname, and it chafed that he'd compare her to a rabbit. Tonight should've proved she was no timid animal, but she'd hopped away as soon as possible.

Demke glanced at her before answering Demetrius, and she read his thoughts in his eyes. She didn't fight, she hadn't taken self-defense courses, and they wouldn't be considering a prison break for John Todd if she'd gone ahead and killed him like most other shifters would've done. "I think she's been through enough with that family."

Relief mingled with shame. She didn't want to be bait. But she didn't want to feel like a burden either.

Jonathan folded his arms, his brows dropping a little. "We'll up security at the prison. And you'll need security."

Everything in her rebelled at the idea. Being followed, her movements monitored, her plans questioned. The thought made her want to throw up. Her stomach churned and a hot flush swept through her body. If she didn't get control of herself, she was going to start sweating, and then they'd all know how much the thought bothered her. She had to be clearheaded.

This was her life and she wasn't going to be bullied out of it. "We're tight on Guardians as it is. I have some ideas about a security detail—"

Demke gestured toward the door where Harrison and Malcolm waited on the other side. "I think the ones we have here would be the best option. They're already extra. I can talk to their commander, but I don't think it'll be a problem to use them for something critical like this."

Her throat constricted so much that when she went to open her mouth, she gaped like a fish.

Demke was not entirely oblivious to what his suggestion was doing to her. "This would be a twenty-four-hour protection detail. We need at least two guards, and we're confident in their skills. Not only do they have a long family history in this area, but their entire lives have been dedicated to protecting us in some way, just like they did tonight."

"Protecting and sleeping with everything that moves, maybe." She clenched her teeth together. Of all the moments for her voice to become fully functional, and she'd said that? But the thought of Harrison trailing her everywhere while Malcolm seduced anything with a vagina made her sick. Having a security detail was bad enough, but assigning the twins to it made it feel like a punishment.

Demetrius's lips quirked. "As a male who used to resemble that remark, I can vouch for the fact that sleeping around does not make one less qualified for a job, nor will it make them less proficient at it."

Logically, she agreed with him, but they were protecting *her*. If they'd been talking about anyone else, she wouldn't bat an eye. No matter her personal feelings about either twin, she would pick them first for any protection detail. But Harrison didn't need to see that she was just as afraid and alone as she'd been when he opened her cellar door.

And wasn't that the rub? That the twins who went out every night and woke up to someone different every morning also excelled at their job. She held their irreverent attitude and flippant behavior against them when she struggled to live her quiet, boring life. Taking solace in the fact that she was good at her job was harder when the twins could do both.

"I just think that there are other candidates we should consider." That sounded professional enough. Though it'd sound better if she hadn't just argued that there weren't enough bodies to do everything the Synod required.

Jonathan spoke quietly. "But would you be willing to

share your history and what happened with those others? The twins are already involved."

He had a damn good point. Her history was already murmured about among their ranks. But since the Synod headquarters was isolated and surrounded by rugged hills, wannabe mountains, and evergreen trees that rivaled skyscrapers, she could ignore the smattering of gossip that didn't leave city limits.

The twins were known as much for the quality of their work as for their playboy reputation. If they were tasked with training, it was thorough and comprehensive. If they were sent on an investigation, they got answers in the shortest amount of time possible. They played hard, but it was off the clock.

Looked like her decision had been made for her.

HARRISON COUNTED each gray hair on Demke's head to keep from looking at Sylva. He and Malcolm stood in front of the head table as if they were discussing a need for additional funds for sparring gear. Out of the corner of his eye, he noted Sylva's cool regard was back in place. A false front. How had he never seen it before?

Demke continued with the list of instructions. "We'll let Sylva debrief you about the brothers and their history. Meanwhile, Jonathan and I will notify the Guardians here to be on the lookout for them."

Jonathan nodded and Harrison was grateful to turn his attention from Sylva. "I will touch base with the West Creek Guardians and let Commander Fitzsimmons know that your presence is required here for longer than previously expected."

Harrison hadn't minded being loaned out here so much

in the last few years, but now he'd rather go back to West Creek and forget about that terrified gleam in Sylva's eyes. He'd never been one to care about others' opinions of him. He was the grumpy twin, the one some were even scared of. His mood was as dark as the look on his face, but he wasn't cruel. But the look in Sylva's eyes when he'd opened that door had made him feel as bad as all the rumors said he was.

Malcolm would sense his unease about guarding Sylva. Would he attribute it the same reason for the anger rolling off him? Malcolm's emotions had nothing to do with Sylva personally, but that someone would hunt down a lone female in the middle of the woods. They might not have a warm and fuzzy glow toward Sylva and the way she tended to pretend they didn't exist, but if someone thought they could terrorize her... Not on Malcolm's watch. Not on *their* watch.

Harrison wasn't sure how he felt yet. The way she'd trembled in front of him was imprinted on his brain. That fear. She hadn't been seeing him per se, but he'd been close enough for it to feel personal. And he didn't like it one bit.

It had only been a couple hours ago when she'd looked at him like her own personal nightmare crashing through the cellar door, and now she had to put her life in his hands. If there was irony there, he didn't treasure it.

"I think that's all for tonight," Jonathan said. The male was as chill as always, never stringing out their meetings just for the sake of hearing himself talk. The respect Jonathan had for him and his brother spoke volumes. There was no need to linger here when it was clear the twins would know what to do.

Malcolm addressed Sylva. "We need to stop at our place and grab an overnight bag. Looks like we're moving in."

His brother had tried for a light tone, but from the intensifying scowl on Sylva's face, it had gone over as well as a tornado siren. Sylva shrank in on herself. The movement was tiny, but Harrison caught it.

When she sent a darting look his way, he caught, too, a glimpse of that staggering vulnerability from earlier. Then it was gone, replaced by the cold, hard expression he knew her for.

"Let us go then." She rose and walked stiffly through the chamber and the receiving area, out the double glass doors.

The walk in the damp night air to their pickup was the only thing that saved him from the frigid vibes rolling off Sylva. As they approached the pickup, his gaze caught on the box where they'd dumped John Todd for the drive over.

Malcolm landed on the same conclusion. "We'll swing by the automatic car wash before we go to our place."

"A little blood doesn't bother me." Her tone was defensive.

"Doesn't it?" The words—and a disbelieving growl—were out of Harrison's mouth before he could think them through. "The male hunted you down and you're saying that the scent of his blood won't bother you?"

She leveled her stare at him, but he caught her hard swallow. "Why don't you think I would relish it?"

Malcolm cut through the tension, like he always did, the lifelong buffer to Harrison's caustic attitude. "I think you should. You took that bastard down. I could leave it messy, a driving billboard announcing 'Don't fuck with Sylva.' "

She blinked, but the sincerity in Malcolm's words did the trick. "A wash would be fine. The scent would only invite questions."

And she didn't want anyone in her life. Her lone existence in the middle of the woods made that clear. They were a pack-minded people. Even he and Malcolm had found a pack to be a part of after they'd left home. At the time, they'd wanted credibility. Working for the same pack that had protected their father would have diminished any good they did, and possibly interfered with Father's work buffering the damage the Lycan Council inflicted. He hadn't done enough and that was why he was in prison, so the pack arrangement had been fortuitous. Harrison and Malcolm were never as involved with the West Creek Guardians as they could be, but it was better than nothing.

"The works, coming right up." Malcolm palmed his keys and unlocked the vehicle.

Sylva hesitated over whether to crawl into the front or the back.

"You're in the back," Harrison said, for once wishing he could speak without sounding pissed off. "You can duck down if we run into trouble."

Sylva's shoulders tightened, but she got in. He went around to the other side and ignored the steady look Malcolm gave him. He didn't have to see it to know it was a combo of "Maybe lighten up a little" and "If she hadn't been through hell tonight, I'd be a little salty about this assignment too."

The drive to the car wash was quiet. Malcolm would start rambling soon. He didn't do uncomfortable silence and had taken on the task of peacekeeper in their family at a young age.

Once the spray shot out of the nozzles, his brother twisted in his seat. "This might be a good time to fill us in on the brothers."

Sylva's complexion paled. No doubt she had been hoping her enemies would just charge into her space so he and Malcolm could smack them down before she was required to open up. She stared at the water-streaked glass, her tone emotionless. "My mate was a bastard who believed everyone was meant to serve his whims. He also took out his every grievance on me until I became little more than a prisoner."

"And he was your mate? Or were you sold to him?"

Her expression tightened. "Natural mates."

Ouch. She must have wondered what she'd done to deserve him.

Malcolm was the one who averted his gaze. "Some of us understand that finding your natural mate doesn't mean happily ever after. Sometimes, they're just a shitty person." Or self-absorbed, in the case of Malcolm's mate. Neither one of them had had a good experience in the mating game. In Malcolm's case, he wasn't at fault, no matter what he thought.

Sylva's lush lips curved into a sympathetic smile. "Yes. Some of us understand. All too well."

"How long were you mated?" For the first time in years, Harrison wasn't content to let Malcolm do all the talking.

Sylva returned to her cool aloofness. "Five years."

"What was the precipitating event after all those years?"

She paused so long he wasn't sure she'd answer. "When he couldn't get me with child and further shackle me to him, he mentioned that maybe his brothers could do the job. It wasn't an idle threat."

A low growl rumbled out of his chest. Sylva pressed into the door. He cut off the noise. She had to know that he wasn't a threat to her, didn't she?

Or did she? She didn't know him and she hadn't wanted to. "Would you prefer a female protection detail?"

She barked out a rough laugh. "Right? You would think so, but no. Not only do I not wish to share my story more times than I have to, but I also don't want those looks. Those 'I never would've put up with that' looks, or those 'I'm too strong to ever tolerate that type of treatment' eye rolls. I had more than enough of those from Roman's sister."

"Fair enough." Malcolm was still turned in his seat. "But you don't seem to like us very much."

"Do I seem like I like anyone very much?"

His brother laughed, but Harrison saw beneath her bravado. She was scared. Of them? Their very presence unnerved her, and it wasn't only because she found their nightly activities disdainful. They were shifters who could hurt her if they chose to, and she'd been around other shifters who had hurt her merely because they could.

CHAPTER 3

"Do we need to bring extra bedding?" Malcolm called from down the hall. The twins' flat was exactly the bachelor pad she'd expected. Little decoration on the walls. A heap of dirty laundry by the door. A mishmash of furniture and a pile of dishes in the sink—but they were clean, at least, set there to dry.

"I have two spare rooms and extra bedding." It had come with the place. Otherwise she wouldn't have bothered to furnish the spare rooms at all. She'd hesitated to purchase the cottage because it was larger than she needed. All that space and she hadn't planned on visitors of any sort.

Crossing her arms, she perched on the edge of the couch. It was softer than it looked—and it looked like it should be waiting by a Dumpster. It had to be older than the building. She had tried to wait by the door, but Harrison had curtly informed her to "stay away from the doors and windows."

When he'd asked if she wanted a female protection detail, she'd almost shouted her answer. *No thank you.* Her feelings on that subject originated with her mate's sister and the perma-snarl she'd worn whenever Sylva had visited.

Shawna had known full well what her brother had been doing to her.

Then there was the rest of their clan, who'd had the same opinion as Shawna. And there was herself. Seeing her own opinion of herself echoed in the eyes of others? There was a reason why she lived alone.

Harrison packed a black overnight bag while Malcolm rattled off their packing list and rifled through cupboards.

An unmistakable scent tickled her nose and she sneezed. Darting upright, she put distance between herself and the couch. But standing by the kitchen counter that separated the main room and the kitchen didn't help.

"Is there anywhere you two haven't had sex in here?" she snapped. The musky odor of hormones and pheromones hadn't faded enough for her taste. And what was she doing sorting through the smells for Harrison's particular scent?

Harrison continued packing his bag, unperturbed. "It is our home. Where else would we have sex?"

"A restroom always works in a pinch." Malcolm seemed to want to lighten the mood, but he only filled her head with random images that made her hot and achy. "I had the pickup detailed last month, or you would've been sneezing up a storm." She was backing up to a bare section of wall to spare her own hormones when Malcolm gave her a sympathetic smile. "You don't want to stand there either."

Harrison froze, his gaze slowly climbing up her body, then to the wall. The shirt in his hand got shoved into his bag.

"You must have so many good memories together." Pure sarcasm poured out of her.

"I don't remember any of them," Harrison said so low that the vibrations rolled right through her with the words.

What would it take for him to remember?

She mentally shook herself. Harrison's sex life was none

of her business, nor any of her interest. She might have to keep reminding herself of that until her brain got it. All she had to do was recall her past with her mate and his brothers. Harrison was gruff like Roman, and for all she knew, Roman had slept with just as many others during their time together —per week—as Harrison.

Her mate's lovemaking could be tender, but it had also been one more way to mentally control her. After a particularly nasty bout or argument, he'd come to her with his figurative tail between his legs and those puppy-dog eyes and tell her how much he loved her and how sorry he was. As the days stretched into weeks and those weeks stretched into months, his story changed after each fight. The subtle insinuation started that it was her fault. That she was lacking. That if it weren't for her, their fight wouldn't have happened.

And when he fucked another female, it was because she was bad in bed.

A hot flush crept up her neck and her face. Those claims had gutted her. Then there was the one time she'd boldly informed him that she'd only ever had one sex partner, so if she was bad at it, perhaps it was her teacher's fault.

She'd worn those bruises for a full forty-eight hours before they'd faded entirely.

When she brought herself out of her memories, she caught the twins looking at her. She was standing in the middle of the apartment, staring at the floor.

"What?" The word came out of her mouth like a whip.

In the Synod chambers her tone would've sent everyone but her fellow Synod members scurrying. But Malcolm only raised a brow and Harrison scowled at her from under his dark eyebrows. The male's beard gave him a more dangerous vibe than was reasonable.

But danger wasn't what she felt when he was around.

"I think we're all packed. We should stop at a grocery

store before we get to your place." Malcolm shoved a hand through his shaggy hair and of course it landed in an artful arrangement. "I doubt you have enough to feed the two of us for a day, much less a couple of months or however long this takes."

A couple of months? For once she wanted Roman's brothers to be competent at a task and get this over with to spare her the humiliation.

"Yes, a grocery store visit would be necessary." There, she sounded calm and collected. But the way Harrison studied her said he didn't buy her act one bit.

UNPACKING THE GROCERIES, Harrison wished he could quit being surprised every time he opened the cupboard. Short of being alphabetized and labeled, these were the tidiest cupboards in the nation. Either Sylva organized her home for a good time or she was so tightly wound up that any disorder threatened to tip her off the edge she teetered on.

Next to him, Malcolm unloaded steaks, hamburgers, and more bacon than a human could consume in a lifetime. "We might need to buy a beer fridge."

"Just how long do you plan on this taking?"

"A lot longer now that those brothers probably know we're here." He spoke low to keep Sylva from hearing. She had retired to her bedroom for the night. "If they waited this long, they're willing to attack her as one of the Synod. They're not gonna be stupid about how they go after her. I wouldn't be surprised if they picked the doofus brother as the guinea pig just to fill her full of fear so she could live in a state of anxiety while they plan the rest of their attack. They likely want her to suffer."

Harrison ducked his head, wishing he were clear minded

enough to think strategically. Instead, he'd been looking at his and Malcolm's place through her eyes. It was little more than a sex den. The way she'd sneezed and looked around like she wanted a bath just because she'd stepped through the doorway had filled him with unexpected shame. Not for how he lived, but for how he'd gotten there. If he'd been stronger, if he'd done more, things would've been radically different.

But then after Sylva had made known exactly what she thought of them and their extracurricular activities, the feeling that had rolled off of her was one he couldn't identify. But he'd wanted to. She hid a lot, just like she hid from her past.

Malcolm was right. If those brothers were anything like her mate, they were playing mind games with her. Those would be harder to protect her from.

All of the groceries were put away, the fridge was filled, and the freezer was stocked full of so much meat they could hardly shut the lid. It was time to officially start work.

"So how do we work our shifts?" Malcolm crossed his arms and leaned against the counter. At least one of them was thinking about the mission and not just the shifter they were protecting. "There's an extra bedroom up here and one downstairs."

"I'll take the ground floor one." He refused to look at his brother. If they were protecting anyone else, Harrison would have fought Malcolm for the bedroom farthest away from their charge. He shouldn't have opened his big mouth.

"And I've got the basement." Yeah, his twin knew something was up, and he also probably sensed that Harrison didn't understand either and figured it was best to ignore it for now.

Mind on the mission. "Twelve-hour shifts. I'll go first."

That would give him the night, when no one else was up. He had some sense of self-preservation. Sylva got to him in a way he couldn't explain, in a way he shouldn't want to explore so much. Taking watch when she would be sleeping was the best idea. But he wasn't giving up the room next to her.

Malcolm pushed off the counter. "I'll be up at noon, then we'll switch to eight-to-eight shifts. We'll figure out any trips to town or when she needs to go in and sit on the Synod later."

It'd give him something to think about through the dawn and into the early morning. Sylva should sleep until close to noon—if she slept at all.

Malcolm disappeared into the basement. He was alone now. If he had to spend the whole time inside this house, he was going to go crazy. Perimeter checks outside the house and sweeps through the nearby woods would be necessary at least once or twice each shift. His twin would know that was part of the plan. Neither one of them would be getting solid sleep till the Raymores were all caught and put away. Or worse. It sounded like they deserved worse.

Blistering fury built up inside of him. Shifters who used their position to intimidate and bully others should be the last ones in power. He wasn't going to let another person get swept up in their particular type of bloody destruction. He would gladly rip apart anyone who came after Sylva, just like he had the ones who'd killed Gloria.

Brimming with the restless energy thoughts of Gloria always evoked in him, he glanced outside. He could burn it off checking the surroundings. Even more if he shifted and ran.

He yanked his shirt off and was mid fold when Sylva's bedroom door swung open. She stopped abruptly, her gaze plastered to his bare chest. Appreciation lit her eyes. He wanted to puff his chest out like some sort of damn caveman. She stepped back into the shadow of her bedroom entry.

"Oh, I—I didn't realize you were changing. I would think you would do that in your bedroom?" She gestured to the door adjacent to hers, as if he couldn't find the spare bedroom.

"Perimeter sweep." He should say more. As he tried to look in her direction without staring, it hit him. She'd transformed herself into a seemingly formidable person, but her default setting was timidity. And she realized when she showed it, but it was like she couldn't help herself.

His respect for her rose a notch. It was hard to change, especially if you were trying to be better and stronger than before, and doing it after you felt like you'd been pounded to nothing.

"Outside?" She winced and her full lips pursed. Her gaze was darting everywhere but at him, until it finally settled in the direction of the front door. "Of course. I mean— Anyway, thanks for letting me know so I know what the noise is."

He could've made sure she never heard a thing, but she probably wasn't a heavy sleeper, thanks to her history.

He should get going, but his boots wouldn't move. "I'm taking the night shift and Malcolm's taking the day shift."

Look at him. He'd become a chatty motherfucker in the middle of the night.

A few awkward heartbeats went by and neither one of them moved. She was so tired that there were dark circles under her eyes that her body wasn't healing.

Since his presence seemed to bother her, he stalked to the front door, opened it quietly, and stepped out into the warm, humid night. The scent of rain hung on the air. Another shower was heading their way. He'd need to finish his check before then. He couldn't come back into the house smelling like wet dog, and he planned on getting back into his jeans before reentering the house. Shifters weren't usually shy about their nudity, but the way Sylva had behaved in the cellar wasn't far from his mind. He'd have to talk to Malcolm about that, too. His twin could walk through the town square nude and pose like a marble statue.

The run was exactly what he needed. The only unrelated scent he picked up was of John Todd, but no other shifter. Trotting back to the little cottage, he changed course to search the yard. Trees crowded the place, giving it excellent shade against the summer sun but enough room to have a sizeable yard. There was a little patch of abundant green growth beside the garage. As he got closer, he could make out the stakes in the ground, neat little signs, and rows. Rows upon rows of various plants. A garden.

Sylva had grown and processed all those canned goods herself? She carried herself with such sophistication, he'd expected to see her wielding a designer handbag, not a pressure canner.

The garden was larger than he'd originally thought. There were actually two sizable gardens. Some plants were blossoming and others had pods lining viny strands. Shifters were the epitome of *meat and potato, but leave the potato* eaters. Their time among humans had varied their taste to include more than just raw meat, but many of them still preferred their cuts rare and their grains in the form of beer only.

In the other garden, he recognized rhubarb. A pang of longing hit him. What the hell was that about?

Homesickness. Since when did he miss a single thing about home?

Since the canopy of rhubarb leaves reminded him of how his sister used to swat him and Malcolm with them. He brought his mind back to the plants.

The answer to what Sylva did in her downtime was obvious. This plot had rows of pokey raspberry bushes, and next to the rhubarb were strawberry bushes that were full of tiny wild strawberries.

Strawberry rhubarb pie. Why did he suddenly remember the dessert? His mom had made it often, the one exception to their protein-heavy diet.

He fucking loved strawberry rhubarb pie. Wait till he told Malcolm about this.

He shook his head. And then what? Were they going to ask Sylva to whip together a pie while they were here? This was business. And no one would be asking Sylva to bake a damn thing.

He was never this nostalgic. To bring up strawberry rhubarb pie with Malcolm and watch him process the memories? No, thanks.

He went back to the porch and shifted into his human form. Once he had his jeans pulled on, he entered the house as silently as he had left it. Sucking in a deep breath, he tried to tell if Sylva was still awake and out of her room. Her scent hung around the house, as it should. But she must be in her bedroom. He treaded back into the kitchen and shrugged into his shirt.

So that had taken an hour. What to do with the next eleven? His gaze landed on the closed door of Sylva's bedroom, and the compassion he'd felt earlier heated into something he didn't care to identify.

This was going to be a long assignment.

"Hey, do you ever make strawberry rhubarb pie?" Malcolm's voice held more than a little excitement. He was creeping along her line of rhubarb plants, his expression reminding her of little kids when they spotted a fresh batch of Maw's baking.

Sitting back on her heels, she brushed the back of her hand across her sweaty forehead. The last two days had been the longest of her life. She'd finally ventured out to her garden to achieve some sense of normalcy only for Malcolm to continually interrupt her with exclamations over what she grew and questions about what she did with her produce.

But the really irritating part was that she didn't mind as much as she should have. "I have frozen some rhubarb, but this stuff is past its season."

Malcolm was nodding as he moved over to the strawberry plants. "Do these things keep fruiting all summer?"

"Depends how much the birds want to incite my wrath." She went back to her weeding.

Malcolm's chuckle was pleasant. He was definitely the

more easygoing twin. She should be having inappropriate feelings about *him*.

The Synod had paused business for as long as possible, taking care of what they could without her. That had left her to hide in her room. And she had, the first night. For twelve hours. She'd never slept that long, but any more nights like that were going to make her rage. The pressure was building inside of her, a longing for the freedom of the forest, but she was too scared to walk outside her door at night and accidentally see Harrison's broad, sculpted chest again.

No wonder the twins never lacked for company. Between their looks and Malcolm's magnetism, she empathized. That wasn't something she could have admitted to before. But knowing that Harrison was on her porch, naked, every night? She'd spent way too long pondering that subject already.

The weeds were ripped out of the soil without mercy. Malcolm squatted to help and while she didn't mind his presence, she'd rather he didn't touch her garden. But it was Harrison she should want to stay far away from. His closed-off personality, his shuttered gaze. He didn't care what anyone thought of him.

Was that why she was obsessing over him? Unlike Roman, Harrison didn't need to constantly prove himself. Unlike her, he didn't put on a show every day of his life.

Malcolm's muscles bunched and flexed as he grabbed another handful of crabgrass. "So do the weeds ever get scared of you?"

The lightness in his tone prompted her to chuckle. "That's not my ability, thankfully, so I can weed to my heart's content."

He rose and went back to patrolling the garden, his gaze jumping from her yard to the trees beyond. "Now that we've been at this a few days, is there anything you need?"

Nothing he cared to hear. How about his twin staying in the basement instead of him? Then maybe she wouldn't try to catch a whiff of Harrison's dewy, night-laced scent each time she walked into her bedroom.

Was his chest as hard as it looked? Was sex with him as rough as she imagined?

So inappropriate, but there it was. Those long nights in her bed with his scent lingering in her house, yes, she'd wondered. There was nothing soft about Harrison, and for some messed-up reason, that made her curiosity even more insatiable.

Roman had been at his roughest when he went fast, but the silver lining had been just that—he'd finished quickly. After Roman had strayed from the bounds of their marriage into other females' beds, she'd given up on trying to please him. Shortly after that, it had become about survival. She had allowed him into her bed without a fight, which had sucked some of the satisfaction out of it for him. That was when the threats about handing her over to his brothers had started.

"Don't you run?" Malcolm was relentless. If she didn't answer him honestly, he would keep picking at her with questions. Again, instead of being annoying, it was an endearing trait. She wasn't used to having someone care about her. And while she wasn't attracted to Malcolm, and despite the way she'd felt about him before all this started, she was growing fond of him.

"I usually run at night. Sometimes I don't sleep very well and I'll wander outside to take a stroll through the trees. But that doesn't seem like the best idea right now."

"We can make it happen. Just talk to Harrison."

She paused and glanced up at him.

The corner of his mouth perked. "Or I'll talk to him." He squinted at the house, where his twin was sleeping. "He's not a bad guy."

"I wasn't questioning whether he was or not."

"You'd be the only one." His eyes twinkled. "But really, he takes his job as a Guardian seriously. He won't let anyone suffer if he can help it. He doesn't make small talk and he doesn't tolerate BS. Don't hold it against him."

"You mean just like I don't like to make small talk and I don't care to put up with anyone's BS, which doesn't make me a frigid bitch?"

He chuckled. "But you have a reason for acting the way you do, correct?"

Touché. What had Harrison gone through to make him the way he was? "I'm a big girl. I can talk to him."

"If you don't want to—"

"It's fine." The twins had been treating her like a cracked vase they were afraid could shatter, and while she appreciated it, it didn't do her any good. The more tender and considerate they were, the more she worried about reverting back into that cowering form in the corner. "Why strawberry rhubarb?"

"What's that?" His brows lifted as if the one-eighty in conversation had taken him off guard. Or maybe he was embarrassed to talk about pie.

"I've been around you long enough to know your eating habits." They practically snarled at her swiss chard and neither one seemed to have a sweet tooth. She was almost to the point of hiding in her pantry and digging her canned peaches out by hand to gobble them down. Her sweet tooth was bigger than her canines. "I'm just surprised that you seem thrilled by the prospect of strawberry rhubarb pie."

"Our mom used to make it, and believe me, if you knew our mother, you'd find that fact astonishing." He grinned, but there was sadness in the depths of his brown eyes. "It just brought back a memory, that's all."

"So if I told you that I had rhubarb frozen and that I think there's enough strawberries to whip together a pie, you'd pass?"

His eyes popped wide. "No, not at all. Please." Then he narrowed his gaze on her, the corners of his lips curving up. "You're messing with me?"

"Busted. But I wasn't messing with you about the pie. I can make one later."

"I don't know if you'll look at me the same way afterward." He sounded so boyish.

The screen door slammed. She and Malcolm swung their heads around to look at the house. A glowering Harrison stomped down the steps. Her heart rate spiked, but not like it usually did when she heard boots thud. Her gaze was riveted to his wide shoulders and the defined chest tapering to his waist. And those thighs. Harrison radiated power with each step.

"She's making us pie!" Malcolm acted oblivious to his twin's mood.

Harrison faltered. "You asked her about the fucking pie?"

Malcolm pointed at the broad leafy greens. "Rhubarb." He pointed to his other side. "Strawberries. Doesn't seem like a large jump."

Harrison's brow dropped further. Instead of being scared, she wanted to laugh. This whole bit about the pie seemed ridiculous, but it obviously meant something to them. Harrison's gaze swung between her and his twin. The weight of his attention didn't lessen. "Why didn't you answer your phone?"

Malcolm touched his back pocket. "No one's been calling me."

"You know they don't call me unless they have to."

Couldn't argue with that logic. She'd heard more than one Synod member paper-rock-scissors who had to call

Harrison if Malcolm wasn't available, but it was such a rare occurrence.

Malcolm dug his phone out. "Ah, man. The battery's dead."

The cut of Harrison's jaw hardened even more. "You're out here without a phone?"

"We went for decades without a phone." Malcolm tapped his head.

Mind-speak. She'd never been close enough to anyone to do it. Being part of the Raymores meant she didn't want anyone in her head. Roman was bad enough.

"Maybe not you." She thought Malcolm was talking to her but he was looking at Harrison. "What did they want?"

Harrison folded his arms across his chest. Sylva went back to weeding, her ears tuned to every word, but she couldn't allow herself to stare at him any longer.

"An update. And to know about her going back to work." Harrison paused, the heat of his gaze skimming across her back. "I told them they should've called her."

Malcolm snorted. "I'm sure they wished they had. Hey, Sylva would like to run at night. How do you wanna do that?"

The burn of Harrison's attention was back on her. She kept her head down. There was never a shortage of weeds.

"You want to run your wolf?" Harrison asked. His tone practically dared her to ask him herself.

Dusting off her hands and standing up, she refrained from shooting Malcolm a dirty look. "Yes, but perhaps we should discuss the Synod first."

Malcolm's full lips turned down. "There's nothing to discuss. Tell us what you want to do."

With two sentences, he'd blown apart how she'd expected their time together to go. If she'd left her room before now, she'd have known that they weren't here to strong-arm her—

or to treat her like her mate and his pack had. "Be careful, Malcolm, or I'll have to admit that I was wrong about you."

Harrison's eyes flared and Malcolm's cheeks grew a faint blush.

He didn't hear that often. She should tell Harrison the same thing, but she couldn't bring herself to. "I usually run at night, sometimes once or twice, depending on how well I sleep. I understand you will have logistics to figure out. Same with the Synod. If they need me there, I can go, but only at your discretion."

Was that a gleam of approval in Harrison's eyes? He glanced at Malcolm. Sylva thought he'd speak, but he left it up to his twin.

Malcolm seamlessly took his cue. "We'll vary the times, skip nights randomly, but it should be fine. With both me and Harrison patrolling, we'll know when they get within a mile of us."

HARRISON WAS IN A SOUR MOOD. First he'd been woken up early thanks to Malcolm's dead phone battery, then he'd walked outside to watch his brother and Sylva giggle together. She wanted to run her wolf at night and had asked *Malcolm*.

But why not run during the day when his twin was on?

So, yeah. He had her run to get ready for. He'd done one sweep of the trees. All clear. It was always possible that Rafe and Clayton could sneak up on them, but he had his doubts.

Before retiring for the night, Malcolm had passed on to him that Sylva would wait inside and Harrison could get her when his perimeter check was done. He was faced with the dilemma of shifting back to his human form and striding into the house naked to notify her or barking and possibly waking Malcolm up. Or he could go through the pain-in-the-ass routine of getting his pants on only to shed them again after she came outside.

A bloody Sylva who was afraid to stand up naked around him passed through his mind.

The pain-in-the-ass routine it was. He hoped she wasn't in her bedroom. That's where her scent was concentrated the strongest. He was becoming accustomed to it.

What a lie. He'd never get used to being surrounded by her soft floral smell. If he could give her smell a color, it would be light pink, like the edge of the early morning sun. He would never be able to see a sunrise and not think of her, and he blamed this shift work. Malcolm wasn't up and ready for his turn until after Sylva woke for the day and ventured out of her room in flannel shorts and a cotton tee.

He couldn't quit stealing glances, hating that he noticed stuff like whether she'd put a bra on or not. Once Malcolm's boot hit the top stair, Harrison had taken to using the bathroom and going straight to his bedroom. As if his minty toothpaste could keep flowers and sunrises from haunting his dreams.

He poked his head through the door, his gaze landing on her immediately. He never had a problem locating her in her room. But that was because her cottage was small. Surely that was it.

All he did was nod and she rose. Her petite body was swaddled in a silky robe instead of her shorts and baggy T-shirt. The robe only accentuated her curves, hiding nothing, yet showing even less.

He'd never given much thought to his type before. Female was his type. His true mate had been brutally murdered, so he wasn't looking for a relationship. But when Sylva's hips swayed by him, he suddenly knew his type was lush curves in a compact form with a smile that had to be earned.

When had he become a damn poet?

She was outside and he was standing in the doorway, letting the bugs in. He strode out to the lawn and turned his back toward her. She wasn't doing anything.

Of course not, fuck nut. She doesn't read you like your twin. "I won't look."

"I appreciate it." She spoke so softly he almost missed what she'd said. That she'd said it in the first place meant she didn't take his gesture lightly.

Her scent floated across him, carried on the night breeze. Was it actually stronger outside? He couldn't help but take a deeper breath. Excitement. She must be going stir-crazy being cooped up in her cottage for days, but she never complained. Other than her initial hesitance to have them as her bodyguards, she had been the perfect client. Like with the work outside. She always asked ahead of time. Tonight, she hadn't demanded to run wherever she wanted. She hadn't argued with either of them about any decision regarding her care.

The faint crunch of grass reached his ears. She had shifted and was walking toward him. Her wolf was short, too, not quite to his waist. Shifter females were often tall, but not Sylva. He could tuck her under his arm and she'd fit perfectly. Not that he'd thought about it.

Spinning on a heel, he went to the porch and shucked his jeans. Shifting into his wolf, he embraced the change. Shifting was as natural as breathing. He'd been doing this each night, more than a couple times. Yes, she must be vibrating out of her skin. And she'd said nothing about her discomfort.

He kicked his chin up, letting her know she could take the lead. Malcolm had informed her that she should stay well within a mile radius of the cottage. Beyond that, he would trail her.

Her wolf was nearly black, blending with the shadows, and likely why she preferred to run at night. She could hide in plain sight. His own wolf was various shades of brown. He knew that without needing a mirror—Malcolm's wolf looked the same.

She sprinted through the trees like it was her job. He didn't have to go full speed to keep up with her, but the run was more effort than he usually put into a relaxing night-time exercise. There was nothing relaxing about her pace other than the expenditure of restless energy.

He expected her to use a set path, but she was chaotic. Up and down hills, leaping off overhangs, darting between trees with no set pattern. She was the definition of random. It was like she kept the rest of her life rigidly under control but this was her time to be free of restrictions, free of expectation, free of anything that hinted at any sort of planning. So unlike her alphabetized pantry.

The scent of the forest flooded him. Evergreen trees, fragrant soil, and little wilderness creatures filtered through his brain until one smell raised his hackles.

Sylva gave no indication of slowing down, and the scent grew stronger.

He let out a little bark. She didn't slow. Was she going faster?

He let out a harsher bark. Her head angled back briefly, but she didn't stop. She'd never trust him enough for mind-speak and even if she did, he couldn't let her in. If Malcolm wasn't allowed in his head, no one was getting in.

Sylva slowed to a trot, her tongue lolling out. The smell was stronger and she was *walking*? A damn mountain lion was heading their way and Sylva wanted to stroll?

If she'd been human, he'd swear she was smiling. Circling around to get between her and the smell of the predator, he bared his teeth, ready for danger.

She bumped against him. Golden eyes glittered in the distance. He wanted to shout at her. Couldn't she tell they were being stalked?

She nudged him again, only this time, she stroked along his body. He staggered to the side, shocked at the intimacy of her touch. Their wolves were a part of them, more like a built-in weapon. It was how they took care of Mother Earth. But shifters kept the touchy-feely stuff for human form. They didn't often cuddle or get busy as their wolf. He had no interest in starting.

But Sylva wasn't paying attention to him. Her gaze was focused on the glittering eyes crouched in the trees.

The mountain lion emerged, its large paws landing soundlessly on the forest floor. As the scent of the big cat grew stronger, the natural alarm inside of Harrison remained dormant.

Sylva padded forward, her head lowered to the side. He was about to leap in between her and the cat when the damnedest thing happened. The animal cocked its head and they both swiped against each other, just like two barn cats.

Sylva was friends with a mountain lion?

She glanced back at him, then jerked her head forward. She started running again, the cat keeping up. Bewildered, he charged after them. Malcolm was never going to let him live this down.

The more carefree she was with the cat, the higher his anger ratcheted up. She hadn't heeded his warning. She was playing with a ferocious cat that could slash her carotid open. Was he wrong about her? When shit got real, would she think she knew better and endanger them all—or just get herself killed?

After several minutes of running, the cat veered off and Sylva angled toward her place. She slowed to a trot, giving them a cool-down period before they reached her porch.

Without waiting for her to turn her back, he shifted. She jerked her head away, but once he was back on two feet, he stormed to his pants.

"Go ahead and shift. It's not like I want to look." The words left his mouth and he hated himself for it. He was upset with her behavior, but what he'd said was too close to a personal insult. He never got personal, not even with put-downs.

She appeared next to him, already shifted, and lifted her robe off the hook. "I take it you're not a fan of Nala."

He waited a moment before spinning on her. He wasn't going to get his point across if he got tongue-tied by bare skin. Thinking about Sylva's satiny skin made his tongue feel like a ten-pound brick.

"The cat has a name?" He shook his head. It shouldn't matter, but it did. How did she know the big cat? How often did they run together? Had the first introduction been a little bloody? What was the point of having a mountain lion as a best friend? It'd only been a few days, but unless it was Synod business, no one called Sylva, and she mentioned nobody. He had the feeling she didn't have friends.

Neither did he, but he had Malcolm.

"It's my gift."

A portion of his anger faded. Unlike most shifters, he didn't have an ability. His gift was Malcolm. It was the same with his twin. Neither of them had been granted any special abilities other than heightened senses and the natural strengths of shifter kind. But he and Malcolm could function as one when needed—and maybe they'd been doing too little on their own lately.

"I can't mind-speak with them, but I know how each animal communicates among their own kind."

Once she said it, he realized that she didn't hunt. The extra meat he and Malcolm had bought was a necessity because she wasn't dropping big game out here. "The gardening."

She dipped her head, a subtle lift to her lips. "It makes it hard to hunt, yes. I buy my meat and have developed a healthy taste for fruits and vegetables." Her almost-smile died. "And gardening gives me something to do."

The glimpse of vulnerability was nearly his undoing. What was he thinking? She was a job. She wasn't a future lover. She wasn't his girlfriend. She wasn't even his friend. Sylva ruled their kind. She was his leader, nothing more.

He'd been furious a minute ago, but once she'd started talking, he'd gotten lost in her voice and hung up on any part of her life that she shared. He summoned his ire once more.

He was her bodyguard until eight a.m. and she hadn't listened to him in the field. "I gave you the signal to stop and you kept going."

"Nala would've thought something was wrong."

"Fuck the cat."

She drew back. "Excuse me? I cohabit in this forest with the big cats. I can't afford to get run out because they decide they don't want an unpredictable shifter in their midst."

"Then communicate that I'm in charge."

One dark brow cocked. An unfamiliar emotion snaked through him as she collected herself, her expression rippling from mild displeasure to wanting to hand feed him to the big kitty herself.

Amusement. He was amused by her reaction to his heavy-handedness.

"Perhaps you should piss on me before our next run," she said. "Mark your territory." She stomped up the steps, the effort giving her full hips extra swing.

The front door slammed. He remained where he was. The noise had probably woken Malcolm and he'd have to explain their little argument.

The image of his twin laughing with a crouched Sylva while she weeded her garden wiped out his amusement. Malcolm was the one women flocked to. Harrison's brooding ways might intrigue them, but he wasn't charming enough to get beyond an exchange of names. Females always wanted something more. Even if he offered them great sex for hours and nothing else, they still wanted more. Like a smile. Or a compliment. Fucking was fucking and that was all the act would ever be for him. Because he had nothing left to give them.

His heart had belonged to one other and she'd been killed because of it.

CHAPTER 5

Sylva waited in the backseat. Malcolm came around the front and got behind the wheel. A grumpy, rumpled Harrison running on three hours of sleep climbed into the passenger seat in front of her.

Demke had called. John Todd had given them nothing. Demke had conferred with the others and they'd all agreed: they wanted to see how John Todd reacted to Sylva questioning him. He'd be shackled and she'd have her trusty guards around.

Then Demke had asked how things were going now that she'd been under close watch for a week. She hadn't known how to answer. The days were good. Malcolm was a delight and she couldn't believe she'd once thought ill of him. He might sleep with a lot of females, but she grudgingly accepted that he made no promises and they knew exactly what they were getting—and that included his brother.

The twinge of jealousy was unfamiliar. Probably because it was too close to insecurity. Just because she'd only been with one narcissistic male didn't mean others should limit themselves. Neither did it mean that she was undesirable.

She was just more discerning. At one time, she would've said she was uninterested, which would be appalling to many shifters. Abstinence wasn't a trait they were born with, nor was it encouraged.

Then she'd seen the twins and something about Harrison's guardedness had gotten to her on a cellular level. That he didn't share with anyone the reasons behind his wariness was even worse. Her mate had spoken about her deficits far and wide in their colony. She couldn't have gotten groceries without the whispering. The scorn. The derision. She hadn't been looking for sympathy, but damn.

She'd once equated Roman with power, but he was weak and violent. The twins weren't. They were powerful.

Giving herself a mental shake, she turned her attention to the road and the upcoming task. "What should I ask John Todd?"

Malcolm's lips pressed into a troubled line. "All the usual questions have been asked, but it wouldn't hurt to see his reaction to you asking them again."

She was dying to ask those same questions, even if it was the definition of redundancy. *Why did you come after me? Why now? Where are your brothers? Why are you a piece of shit?*

"Ask him why he doesn't believe in treasuring a mate." Harrison's voice was rougher than usual. "Ask him what pride he gets in brutalizing another. Ask him what his definition of honor is."

By the time she glanced at him in the rearview mirror, his expression had shuttered.

The Synod probably hadn't asked those specific questions, and they didn't have to. "I can answer them for you. Sweet Mother Earth, I've heard the reasons so many times. If I were a strong mate, I could've stood up to him. He didn't attack me, he was teaching me a lesson. How would I get stronger without overcoming adversity? Honor is providing for a mate. Did he not provide me food? Did he not provide me water? Hell, I even got a bottle of wine once in a while. I got to go out with his sister—where I was monitored, of course. I'm the one that lacked honor. I'm the one that wasn't appreciative. I'm the one that couldn't get pregnant."

Bitterness dripped off every word. Five years was a blink to their kind. They lived long lives and were often mated for a century or two before a kid came along. But Roman had had big dreams of building a strong pack to take over the surrounding colonies. He'd just needed the numbers and he'd needed them before his brothers mated and reproduced or he'd end up like his parents—killed by another sibling's young in a scramble for power before Grandma Raymore thumped her cane down and told them how it was going to be.

"That's a seriously fucked-up way of thinking," Malcolm said.

"I was groomed for it." If it weren't for her mother, she would've believed all the nonsense told to her.

"How?" Harrison growled.

Why had she opened that particular door to her past? But it was just the three of them in the vehicle and they knew so much already. Wouldn't it be nice to talk about her life for once?

"I grew up hearing and seeing the Raymores' power. My parents knew that I was destined to be with Roman, so I was taught what the Raymores expected out of a mate. Obedience and reproduction." She'd happily been noncompliant on both accounts.

Malcolm cast a sympathetic look her way. "As Guardians, we see that a lot in the more isolated colonies. One family takes over and any sense of democracy goes out the window.

And they're too far off the beaten path for Guardians to police."

Relieved they weren't going to ask her to spell it out, she said, "Might makes right in their minds, but they conveniently forget that there is supposed to be a system of honor to the shifters' version of might makes right."

"That's why our mother was so unpopular." Malcolm chuckled. "She didn't want anything to do with anyone, but if someone in our colony failed to follow shifter protocol, she stepped in, in a muscle shirt with the sleeves cut off and a cigarette hanging out of her mouth."

"I didn't realize your family led a colony." Their father was serving time in the Synod prison for his role in the previous Lycan Council. His incarceration was mostly for show since he'd been complicit, but not an instigator. His imprisonment was even over, but they couldn't get him to leave.

Malcolm's gaze jerked toward Harrison. "Uh, we weren't the leaders. Maw just had a low tolerance for ignorance, and she protected Father's status."

But there was something they weren't saying. Harrison was rigid in his seat, his body unmoving as the vehicle bumped over the road. Her question had touched a land mine without setting it off.

The Synod's headquarters loomed ahead much sooner than she was ready. Normally, it was a comforting sight. Here she spoke and others listened. She was conscious not to abuse her authority and made an effort to help those like her.

But now she was entering as exactly herself. Sylva Raymore. The shifter female who needed bodyguards.

Malcolm took the circular drive, parked in front of the entrance, and killed the engine. Harrison was out before she was, his dark gaze sweeping the mostly empty parking lot that spanned the length of the building.

Shifters had excellent senses, but they still hadn't planted much shrubbery around this place. The fewer places for someone with ill intention to hide, the better. River rock was the landscaping material of choice, broken up by pops of colorful flowers. This side had no stairs. The other side had one level above ground and one below for the vampires they now had to work with. Prisoners were kept underground, but the Synod conducted much of their business after sunset.

She preferred busy evenings with her early hours full of yard work and gardening. It made her days less depressing. Except, how sad was it that she looked forward to work as much as she did?

When Malcolm headed toward the door, she followed with Harrison trailing after them. The wall of heat behind her didn't make her feel as safe as it should have. The reason for being here loomed before her like a storm cloud. They weaved through the building to the lower level, and it wasn't long before the interrogation room came into view.

Demke was waiting outside, his standard congenial expression absent. "Thanks for coming. I wish we didn't have to resort to this."

"I want to be in the room alone with him." She knew her demand wouldn't go over well.

"No." The terse response came from behind her.

Without looking over her shoulder, she replied, "He's going to use your presence against me. Mentally. These guys have played mind games with people like me their entire lives. I need to use the upper hand while I have it. And that will mean walking into that room as Sylva Raymore, member of the Synod."

"Keep the door unlocked," Malcolm said. "We'll be on the other side."

The twins were quieter than normal. Were they mind-speaking? She'd never noticed them doing it before. Roman and his brothers had only talked telepathically around her. She thought she'd become attuned to the subtle vibrations of mental communication, but not with Malcolm and Harrison.

Speaking to John Todd was something she should have done already. It should've been her idea. That Demke had had to weather the guilt of his decision only weighed on her. "Let's get this done."

Demke stepped aside. A white metal door blocked her from the man whose carotid she'd bitten through a week ago. As she looked at the door, she could only wonder why she hadn't finished the job.

If you were stronger, you would've had what it took to get the job done.

Her mate's words kept coming back to haunt her. Why did she keep defaulting to the thought that he was right?

Shutting the part of her mind off that doubted all of her actions, she opened the door and walked inside like she was royalty.

Lifting her chin until she could look down her nose at John Todd, she studied his appearance. He was just as large as she remembered. His bulk hadn't gone unnoticed when she'd surprised him last week, but she hadn't dwelled on it. All the males of the Raymore pack were large. And they never hesitated to use their size to intimidate. If only she'd grown tall like most shifters, she might not have felt so dwarfed by them in every aspect.

John Todd's bright blue eyes tracked her. She stared hard into their sky-blue depths. Mirth. Arrogance. And maybe just a little doubt. The way she held herself surprised him. Part of her stiffness was the smell. Was he refusing showers or not being offered them?

"I would say it's good to see you again," she started, keeping her mental door firmly shut on her past. She was the new Sylva, not the female this guy had once known. Standing across the table from him gave her the perfect opportunity to look down on him. "But I made it clear the other night how I felt about your visit."

His mouth curled up in a sneer. "I was just stopping by to say hi. Is that how you greet an old friend?"

"You know I have no friends. You guys always made sure of it."

"A strong female would've surrounded herself with plenty of supporters."

There it was. Just like old times. She pulled a chair out and sank into it as gracefully as possible. With her back ramrod straight, she folded her hands on the tabletop. "It was my supporters who dragged you off my porch and dumped you here."

The bastard laughed. His smile died just as abruptly. "I would say that I've missed your fire, but you and I both know that it only came after your act of cowardice." His eyes burned as bright as the hottest part of the flame.

She willed her heartbeat to remain steady before it beat out of her chest like a terrified jackrabbit. "What made you come here to dredge up the past? Roman is dead." Using his same tone, she said, "A stronger male would've moved on."

Fury rippled through his features, extinguishing that fire, making his gaze as cold as a Canadian winter. "Our justice system didn't have a chance to deal with you. I've taken it on myself to right that wrong."

"From where I stand, the justice system in Four Claws is nothing but cowardice. How else would you explain the need for ultimate rule if your family believed it could maintain power in the first place?" She tilted her head to the side, looking at him as if she were studying a bug. That would get under his skin more than any words she could say.

A red flush crept up his neck and into his cheeks. If he got any hotter under the collar, his head was going to pop off.

Maybe his body would whistle like a teakettle. And his sweaty musk would choke her.

She was right and he knew it. In this little room, she was the one with the power. It was refreshing. Too bad she couldn't forget the sheer panic racing through her veins when he'd been on her porch.

He narrowed his eyes. "You think you got me, don't you? Did you forget, little female, that you only killed one of us?"

The corner of her mouth kicked up in a snarl. Roman used to call her "little female," and it hadn't been a term of endearment. "The thing is, I don't have to remember. You and your brothers mean nothing to me. *Nothing.*"

He growled and slammed his fist on the table. It took all her restraint not to flinch.

The door cracked open. As soon as she heard the click, she commanded, "Stop." She had to rescue the situation or John Todd would still think he was right about her. He was, but it was important she put on a good show. "It's just a temper tantrum."

It was Malcolm who chuckled as the door shut. But a glow of appreciation sparked in her belly. She doubted he found anything funny, which meant he'd done it only to get under John Todd's skin. Malcolm was quickly becoming the best friend she'd ever had. What was Harrison thinking?

John Todd had gotten over his bout of anger. He was reclining in his chair, returning the scrutinizing look she'd once given him. "Still the weakest one in the room. Can't protect yourself, can't do anything for yourself, have to rely on some big strong shifter to take care of you."

It was a struggle, but she kept shame from reaching her expression. That tiny voice in her head wanted to scream how true his words were. She hadn't risen to the top because of her own deeds. She'd been placed there because she'd been a victim. Who better to represent other victims in their society? And while she might've taken down John Todd the other night, she'd failed to carry through with any real action. The first moment she'd had a chance, she'd called for help.

But whatever her path to power, she had it now and she wasn't going to shirk her responsibilities. "Still the big strong male who thinks with his fangs instead of that tiny brain rattling around in his head."

Anger vibrated through John Todd but he refrained from lashing out. Leaning forward and resting his elbows on the table, he said in a low, deceptively calm tone, "I can't wait for Rafe and Clayton to teach you how to properly show respect." He moved even closer and she pressed back into her own chair. "When they're done, they'll enjoy telling me all about your little squeals. Especially when they make you beg for mercy you haven't earned."

She would swallow hard, but her throat was as dry as if she'd gargled with sand. This interview couldn't be an abject failure. Demke and Harrison and Malcolm were waiting outside. They'd arranged their entire day around this interview, and the twins were giving up all of their time to guard her. She couldn't crumble under this sorry excuse of a shifter.

She kicked her chin up and borrowed the haughty expression Demetrius often wore. It was like his version of a resting bitch face, and it used to drive her crazy until she'd gotten to know him. Now, she'd mimic him. "And I'll enjoy being the one to tell you that they did not survive our encounter." This time she was the one to lean forward, her voice low. "Maybe I'll even bring their heads in so you can see firsthand what a weak female I am."

She stood and pushed her chair in with deliberate precision. But as she was walking out the door, he said, "I don't believe for one second that you could kill either one of them."

She sensed the twins hovering on the other side of the open door. Those couldn't be the final words. This couldn't be how she left the interview in front of those she respected.

She paused and looked over her shoulder, the lie leaving a bitter taste in her mouth. "What I did to Roman is proof enough."

CHAPTER 6

Harrison awoke to the most delicious smell. He blinked his eyes, then scrubbed his face as he sat up and swung his legs over the edge of the bed. The aroma wrapped around him like a warm blanket.

Was that…pie?

Sylva had said she was fine after her talk with John Todd, but she hadn't been the same. When they'd returned the previous night, she'd gone straight to her room. He and Malcolm had given each other a look and brushed it off. Anyone would need space after a conversation like that. But she'd been more stoic than any female in the comfort of her own home should be.

He was interested to see what Malcolm's report about the day would be. Shrugging into his T-shirt and jeans, his uniform of choice, he stuffed his feet into his boots. Malcolm went all over the place barefoot supposedly in case he had to shift on short notice, but it was more likely that he was just way too comfortable in this little cottage.

Every time he thought of Malcolm and how comfortable he was in Sylva's home, and how much those two seemed to get along the more they were together, he got all…achy. If it had been anyone other than his brother, his twin, he might have let it show. But this was Malcolm, and seeing him happy was too important to Harrison.

Besides, it was ridiculous to think that he was good for anything more than a screw.

His gaze stayed on the doorknob. *Just open it and go out.* But he couldn't.

Malcolm's voice vibrated through the wood. Chatter. Malcolm and Sylva were *chatting*. Sylva didn't say more than three words to Harrison during the night shift, but she and Malcolm were suddenly buds?

He shook his head. This juvenile jealousy was going too far. Malcolm was putting her at ease, which was his job, to protect her while not scaring her worse in the first place.

If he delayed any longer, he'd be late for duty—and he wouldn't know if that delectable smell was really pie.

In the kitchen, Malcolm was leaning against the small square island. The look on his face was one Harrison hadn't seen since they were little boys, and sweet Mother Earth, that smell. It unplugged all his unwanted childhood memories. Good ones.

Memories he should want to remember, but had refused to. No one would think a guy with his personality had had an idyllic childhood, but parts of it had been. Sprinting through the forest, darting around trees, and racing Malcolm home for a slice of Maw's pie right out of the oven… Longing came next. Always the longing. Wanting those days back. The excitement. The thrill for life, for living.

"Just in time for a slice." Malcolm's smile was as broad as Harrison's own answering frown. His brother remained unfazed. "It'll cheer you up."

Unlike him, Malcolm didn't shun recollection of the good times. They didn't haunt him. Or maybe they did, but the suffering was worth a piece of strawberry rhubarb pie. Harrison's gaze strayed to the counter. With fresh fucking whipped cream.

It wasn't just pie that Sylva had spent the day preparing. Five loaves of bread lined the counter, and muffins or cupcakes were set in rows behind them. His nose twitched. Hints of zucchini. She'd done some harvesting and gone straight to baking.

Sylva was a stress baker.

He lifted his gaze and found hers boring into him. She'd been through a tough time and the proof was in the baked goods.

"Smells good." The dark circles under her eyes were enough for him to make an effort. She might've gone straight to bed last night, but he doubted she'd gotten any sleep.

The tension in her expression eased until she looked almost sheepish. "I figured a pie was the least I could do, and I added chocolate chips to the zucchini loaves at your brother's request."

Malcolm gets whatever he wants. Harrison shook the thought out of his head. Hadn't he just been thinking how nice it was to see Malcolm damn near giddy? Malcolm had probably asked nicely and given her that trademark smile. Harrison wouldn't have had the chance because she hid in her room most of the time he was on duty.

What was it about Sylva that twisted him in knots?

Three plates were on the counter, a slice centered on each of them. Rich pink liquid swirled around the base of each piece. Both he and Malcolm were mesmerized as she dolloped whipped cream on top one by one by one. A fork was placed in front of him and in front of Malcolm and a plate slid their way.

Harrison stared at his like it was a viper about to strike. Malcolm had zero hesitation. Sylva lifted her plate and cut the corner of the wedge off with her fork. She scooped her fork under the piece but didn't lift it to her mouth. She was waiting for him.

Just like their mother used to.

"Remember how Maw liked to watch each one of us eat our pie first?" Harrison winced. What had made him ask that?

Malcolm's chewing slowed and his brow crinkled. He answered with a gruff, "Yeah. Camille was always the first to finish."

He worried his brother was going to set his piece down unfinished, but he held on to it. That didn't mean the man wasn't continuing on without great effort.

"Camille?" Sylva lifted the top crust off the piece she had cut and took a bite from it. The move might've riveted Harrison only a minute ago, but the trip down memory lane had snagged his attention.

"Our sister."

Her eyes widened, but she finished chewing. "Oh. I didn't realize you guys have a sister."

"Had," he said quietly. "We had a sister." Then as if the decades-old floodgates had been lifted, he let it all spill out. "She was older than us, and a pain in the ass. But she was the center of our world."

"And she'd love this pie." Malcolm always knew what to say to lighten the mood.

Why had he brought up their sister?

"I'm sorry." The sympathy in her eyes didn't send him running. He clung to it.

"It's okay." And that was something he never said. But it *was* okay. He and Malcolm should talk about Camille more, not pretend that she'd never existed. "She was blond like Maw but had Father's charm. She was the only one who could make Maw laugh."

He shoved a bite of pie into his mouth. It barely fit. But then he hadn't been paying attention to what his fork was cutting into. Sweetness blasted over his tongue, only to be cut through with the unique, bitter flavor of rhubarb. Just as good as Maw used to make. Rhubarb and wild strawberries and an unhealthy amount of sugar combined with an obscene amount of butter in the crust, and he was transported back to the best times of his life.

Malcolm's face was ashen, but he was trying to hide it. For once, Harrison took over to give Malcolm space. "She liked animals. Especially horses, and they never seem bothered by her. Harrison and I can't even look at a horse before it bolts across the pasture, but they'd always come running for her."

"She was special," Sylva said softly.

"She left and never came back."

Harrison jerked at Malcolm's words.

It had been so long since they'd spoken about her, and tonight was like yanking duct tape off a gaping, festering wound.

The story poured out of Malcolm. "She loved riding, just riding forever. So we didn't think anything when she didn't come back for an entire day. But then night fell and even the well-worn trails where we grew up wouldn't be good for the horse. But even still, we were worried about her because of her horse. If anything happened to Barrel Racer, it'd break her heart. And if she felt responsible, it would destroy her."

"But she never came back." Harrison finished off his dessert just to have something else to do besides thinking about the day his sister had vanished.

Sylva folded her hands on the countertop, her plate next to them, the rest of her food untouched. "I'm so sorry. You must've searched forever."

Malcolm snorted. "Our parents worried we'd get lost, too. We didn't quit searching for—"

"Years." Regret clouded his vision until all he could see was Maw explaining what had happened to Gloria. She was the reason they'd finally come out of the woods. He was the reason she was dead.

"No idea what happened?" The gentleness of her voice cleared his mind, but he didn't deserve it.

Sylva made him want things that he hadn't wanted in a long time. He wanted her to curl up with him as he told her about those long nights in the forest, how he and his brother had refused to give up, and how despair had set in as each day went by and they didn't find her. He wanted to describe how her scent had faded to nothing until he and Malcolm had been left hunting and hoping aimlessly.

"She was happy," Malcolm said. "She wouldn't have run away. Hell, she was an adult. She could've moved away whenever she wanted. But she kept saying that she'd move when she found her mate. All we can think is that she got abducted."

Harrison sensed the question before she could ask it. "We don't believe she was murdered. We were never able to get a strong bearing on her scent. It was faint along the trail she'd left on and only grew fainter."

"And your mother and father had plenty of enemies." Sylva might not have known their parents, but she knew *of* their parents. Everyone did. Father had been on the Lycan Council. And their mother… Well, she was Maw.

"Father scoured his list of enemies, but nothing." Malcolm pushed away from the counter. "Thank you for the pie. Seriously. There'd better be a slice for breakfast." He turned to go downstairs. "It was a pretty quiet day. No new scents."

By the time Harrison tore his gaze off his brother, Sylva had busied herself at the sink. She never let them help with dishes, and it was all they could do to clean up after meals without getting shooed away. *You two are already working. You don't need to do extra cleanup.*

Sylva glanced over her shoulder. She was silhouetted by the fading daylight streaming through the window across from her. With her refined features and the slight twist to her body accentuating her curves, he could stare at her all night. "I'd like to go for a walk tonight. As myself, not my wolf."

The last part was a relief. After the recent discussion about his sister and the reminder of those years in the woods, a relaxing stroll would help file the memories back in place. They were currently surging in his brain. The way he and Malcolm had smelled after weeks of searching before they stopped to take a dip in the river. The metallic tang of their rabbit kills. And the smell of the rainstorm when they'd turned around and raced for home. All that needed to go away.

But that left him taking a stroll in the forest with Sylva at sunset. He'd only done that with one other person. His pulse sped up and he swiped a hand over his chest. She was going to sense the turmoil inside of him if he didn't control himself.

"I'll wait outside." All he needed was just a few minutes to gather himself and then he'd be fine.

SHE NEEDED THIS. With the trees, the temperature dropped quicker at night during the summer. It was cool enough to keep from breaking a sweat as she followed the deer trail.

Her thoughts returned to the twins and their sister. She should've known there was more to these guys than she'd first assumed. She should've known that a shifter's past carved out their present.

Still, she couldn't help but think that it was just one part of their story. Losing their sister was tragic enough. Add in the nightmare of not knowing why, and that was all that was needed to change a person. It explained their protective nature, and why they were constantly drawn back to the place where they'd been raised.

But it didn't explain their particular sex life. It wasn't hard to see that they had a routine. They had sex frequently, with several different partners, and they rarely revisited the same one. The twins stayed away from anything that would make their partner think there might be more than sex on the table.

Sex on the table. She smirked, glad that Harrison was behind her. A hot flash crept up her body. *Please don't let him sense my arousal.*

She should thank Harrison. For a long time she'd wondered if she would ever be turned on again. She'd worried that Roman had broken that part of her. And if she wanted to analyze the way she'd judged the twins, it probably had to do with her terrible sexual insecurity.

She was caught between appreciating that the deer trail was too narrow for them to walk side by side and mourning what a nice night it would be to stroll next to each other and chat. There was so much she didn't know about him, and when he'd spoken earlier, it was like a whole different Harrison had walked out of the bedroom.

Was he irritated because she talked so freely with Malcolm? His grumpiness lately had seemed more personal, more pointed. The glares he shot his brother, followed by flashes of recrimination, made her think that he wanted his twin to find happiness and was upset at himself about feeling jealous.

Way to get ahead of yourself. Just a couple of weeks ago, she would've sworn he hated her. She hadn't given him a reason not to. And he probably would've bet all his money that she detested him. And those would've been the words she'd have used.

So much had changed within a week. Yes, she spoke freely with Malcolm, but he didn't tell her anything. He was a master of small talk, an expert at stretching out details and asking a zillion questions but never revealing a thing about himself. Did Harrison know that? Did he know that his brother wasn't open with her?

She had no problem giving Malcolm all the space he needed. It wasn't her business.

Harrison wasn't her business either. But she was definitely having a problem giving him space. She rubbed her tongue along one canine. She was way too curious about his business.

She reached a spot where the trees thinned, and she meandered around the trunks. More grasses grew here, receiving extra rays of the sun thanks to the thin overhead canopy.

"I was walking faster than I intended." She rested her hands on her hips to keep herself from charging ahead. This was supposed to be a relaxing walk after the flurry of the last couple of days.

As Harrison entered the clearing, emerging from the shadows cast by the setting sun, a few fading rays highlighted his face. Gold sparkled in his rich brown hair and danced along his beard. Her fingers twitched to roam through those silky strands, to see how different the texture of his hair was from his beard.

She wouldn't peg him as vain, but he took care of his beard. He kept it trimmed and soft. He was handsome. Good-looking. *Hot.* His dark expressions often gave others the impression that Malcolm was the better-looking twin. They were identical, but at the moment she thought Harrison was ten times hotter than Malcolm.

This walk wasn't relaxing. It didn't appear to be for Harrison either. He seemed tenser than when they'd started, stalking the clearing like the predator he was. The part of him that had unraveled while they were talking over pie was now tightly coiled and bound inside of him. Why?

"Do we need to go back?" she asked. "I don't have to be out."

His brows drew down. "There's no reason to head back."

"I thought perhaps you sensed something wrong. You seem…" She waved her hand up and down at him. "Stressed."

"I am. But not because I sense any danger."

Her heart sank. She dropped her gaze and turned away. She was the one bothering him.

As she was berating herself for allowing her interest to run rampant, a tidal wave of heat slammed into her back. He was right behind her. When she turned, she had to tip her head back. She hated having to look up just as much as she hated needing a stool for the top shelf of her cabinets, but with Harrison, it was thrilling.

"It's not you." His lips formed a troubled line. They looked soft. How would they feel if she pressed her lips to them?

How could he tell that was bothering her? "Me?"

"I'm not upset because of you." His jaw flexed. "Not really."

"So it is me. I understand that we weren't friendly before this started. I had a lot of preconceived notions, and I'm sure you had the same. I just hoped that perhaps we'd gotten past that."

He didn't relax. His shoulders were wide enough and they were standing close enough that he was all she could see. His scent crowded out the forest. Nothing but clean, dewy male at night. "It was easier when I thought I had a reason to dislike you."

If he didn't dislike her, did that mean he *liked* her? Nervous energy sizzled through her veins. Perhaps it was just his proximity, because it'd be sad if she reacted like this just because he didn't hate her. "I don't dislike you anymore either." She called on her boldness. "It's more of the opposite."

"Really?" The confession only sharpened his gaze and made those soft-looking lips turn down. "I can't... You can't... You're my job."

The words cut through her and her energy dissipated like an early-morning fog. "Right. You're right. I need to keep that forefront in my mind." She was about to turn away and give herself a long lecture about professionalism when his hand stroked along her upper arm. He cupped her elbow, rooting her in place.

"I fuck. That's all. I don't flirt, I don't charm, I don't date, and I don't do relationships. You deserve all of that, and you deserve it from a better male than me."

Heat exploded through her body at his words. "Well I appreciate your candor, but I prefer to decide for myself what I deserve and from whom. I believe I've earned that privilege."

She caught his beat of regret. "It would be wrong of me to pretend that there was anything between us."

"You think there could be though?" She inched closer to him, his hand still closed around her elbow. "All this extra fascination I have with you isn't my imagination. You feel it, too?"

He took a full step backward, releasing her. "It doesn't matter. I had this before and it was taken away. It was taken away because—"

She respected his need for space. "I will listen if you care to share."

Debate raged in the depths of his brown eyes. She could guess what had made him decide to start talking. He knew her entire story, and he likely felt bad that he was letting her down without giving her insight into his. "I had a mate once. We were young and we hadn't bonded. She was killed long before that could happen."

She fought the urge to close the distance between them. This confession must take a lot, and he'd already made it plain he wished to keep distance between them. "You've lost a lot in your life." She couldn't hold in her scornful laugh. "It seems both of us have experienced quite a lot in our short lives."

His expression lightened. "Yes. I was guessing we were about the same age."

She was young in shifter years, closing in on thirty. Harrison and Malcolm hadn't hit the half-century mark. But she felt far older than her years, yet young and stupid at being told he didn't want to take a chance on this thing between them.

Having them both here had shown her how lonely she was. She didn't want to lose what they brought to her life. "I'd like to at least be friends."

"You seem pretty friendly with Malcolm."

Yes, she enjoyed her time with Malcolm, but the air between her and Harrison's twin wasn't charged and loaded. "Friendly, yes. But he is quite the master of superficial relationships. And I'm not as curious about him as I am about you."

Instead of a glint of humor, his features darkened. "I'm usually the mystery women want to puzzle out, only to realize that they don't like what they find."

"I'm not like most females," she snapped. Comparing her

to his long line of past encounters was insulting. He hadn't shared the memories of his sister with just anyone. "I don't wish to experience both you and your brother at the same time."

He had the grace to look ashamed. "No, you're not like any female I've ever met."

"And you're not like any male I've ever met. Sorry for my earlier judgments."

He stuffed his hands in his pockets. "Me, too."

They were starting on new footing. Two people who seemed to like each other but couldn't be more. She feathered her hair behind her ear. His gaze tracked the movement. With the sun sinking farther into the horizon, his eyes were starting to glow with the reflective sheen of their kind. Hers were probably doing the same.

"Friends?" she asked, because he was becoming more than a bodyguard.

"Friends." He said the word slowly, like it was a foreign sound his tongue had to get used to.

She doubted Harrison claimed anyone as a friend. Opposites might attract, but she and Harrison were more alike than she'd thought. "Good thing we went for a walk tonight."

The corner of his mouth twitched. She rarely made anyone smile. So to get a mouth twitch from a male like Harrison? It showed just how far she'd come.

"You're right about Malcolm," he said. "I assumed no one noticed."

"Does anyone spend that much time around him without you?"

His answer was in his eyes.

She'd thought so. They were each other's buffer. "It's okay. He'll talk when he finds someone he trusts. And I enjoy the light conversation."

"You don't get that with me."

"I'm getting it now."

His lips quirked again. "My voice might get hoarse if we keep going like this."

Her laughter felt good. So did his twinkling eyes. Everyone liked to point out how different the twins were aside from their appearance, and he probably did the same in his head. But he'd just wielded an ounce of charm so effectively that he could rival his brother in that department. And she was the only one who knew.

She'd like to stay and keep talking, but then it'd feel forced. "Can we walk again tomorrow night?"

"Only if you promise to laugh again." A hint of a smile played along his lips, but the way he looked at her sent a wave of heat rolling through her body. He wasn't teasing her.

"If you'll keep it a secret that I *have* a sense of humor."

"Sylva, your secrets will always be safe with me."

CHAPTER 7

"**I** thought we were going to walk." Sylva's petulant tone made him want to laugh. They were standing in the middle of her yard with a sky packed full of stars above them.

"Since we walked the last couple of nights, I thought we could do this instead." He wanted to hang out alone in the forest with her. The last two nights, they'd gone on one run and then one walk. During their strolls, they'd talked.

The first night, he'd asked her about the garden and he'd gotten more information on vegetable planting and her canning calendar than he'd bargained for. He'd hung on every word. Last night, she'd asked about what it was like growing up with a twin.

Stories of his childhood had spilled out like she'd rubbed a genie lamp. He told her about the time he and Malcolm tried drag racing on the highway and caught the attention of human police. It'd taken Father's interference, calling in special favors from others shifters to use their abilities, to get the whole thing dropped.

Tonight, he wanted nothing more than to hear the sweet

chimes of her laughter and know that he was the cause. Him. Harrison Wallace, professional brooder.

He never made anyone laugh. Gloria had been so worried about everything that he couldn't get through to her. But unlike Gloria, Sylva was already in a position of power and willing to fight for it.

And that's where his idea had come from. He hadn't known how she'd receive it, but it wasn't looking good. Were three walks enough for her to trust him?

"I thought I could show you some moves. Self-defense moves."

She arched a dark brow. "Oh, really?"

"We noticed you never attend."

She looked away. "It wasn't because I don't think they're good courses."

"It was because of who taught them."

Guilt reflected in her eyes. "Not exactly."

"Can I work with you now?"

Her gaze danced around the yard as if seeking refuge. "I don't know that I'm comfortable with that."

He could guess where her additional hesitance was coming from. If she'd gotten over who her instructor was, then it must be what he would be teaching. "I won't lay a hand on you."

"It's not that." Her gaze met his. A million stars shone in her eyes, making them luminous. And revealing her vulnerability. "I'm not scared of you, Harrison." She paused, her brows knit. "I'm known for being tough, but not vicious. I created my new life around the idea that I wasn't like my mate and his family. I was different."

That she was better. She didn't have to say it, but it clarified why she didn't like violence. He couldn't tell her to just embrace her shifter side. She'd had to embrace everyone else's her entire life.

He mulled over the issue. It wasn't as simple as letting her off the hook, saying *no problem, we'll work around it.* Her life was in danger.

He wasn't giving up. "Self-defense isn't about being ready to fight. It's about learning the skills that you would *choose* to use if the time ever came. How about you tell me what you wished you knew the night John Todd was here?"

The crease between her brows deepened, but she considered his words. Her expression softened and the corner of her mouth crept up. "I actually thought about how I skipped those damn courses that night. I wished I'd gone to every one."

"We can help you catch up. Our lessons include fighting in wolf form, too."

She sighed and glanced at the house. "How about I do a session with you at night and one during the day with Malcolm?" She chewed on the corner of her lip. "But no firearms."

"No firearms." He understood why she'd have a hang-up about guns. It was more critical she learned to fight with her hands and teeth—and her claws. Then they'd work on firearms, since she still had a pistol loaded with silver-laced bullets under her roof.

"Should I change?"

She was wearing leggings that hugged her like a second skin and a baggy T-shirt that played peekaboo with the curves of her hips. No, he didn't want her to change, but she also wouldn't need to.

"No. We can work our wolves tomorrow night, unless Malcolm wants to teach you."

"Okay. Where do we begin?"

SYLVA KICKED, aiming straight for Malcolm's gut. He deflected and lunged for her again. She punched like he'd taught her. Throat. Nuts. Throat. He caught each one like he was wearing a catcher's mitt.

"Good. Ready to shift?"

He'd asked yesterday, but hand-to-hand was easier. She imagined Roman's sneering face, heard his words in her head. *A stronger female would...*

But shifting reminded her too much of John Todd. "I think I can do okay as my wolf." She had already, after all. Getting used to the lessons hadn't been as hard as she'd thought. It was a physical release, just like hours of canning, but more innate. It came naturally and that bothered her.

Skills you would choose *to use...* That made all the difference.

But he didn't buy her excuse to skip shifting. "What happens when it's two of them and you don't have the element of surprise?"

Dammit. "Fine."

"If you're more comfortable waiting until tonight with Harrison, that's fine with me. I just want you to practice."

Harrison was a good instructor. He went at her pace, which was much faster than she'd expected. And he'd been true to his word. He mimed the moves and didn't touch her until they got started with practice. Then he was always on the receiving end, catching her hits as deftly as Malcolm. Her kicks, too. The twins seemed indestructible, but instead of feeling weak, she was empowered in a way she'd never thought she could be.

"It's not who works with me. It's that..." She didn't want to panic and run to her house and hide in front of them.

"You're afraid you can't overcome your fear."

"Harrison saw me like that and I—" She shook her head. "You and I should practice."

"Let's walk through it. Say you and Harrison shift and he snarls just like John Todd did and you run away. Then what?"

She bit the insides of her cheeks. Her eyes burned like she wanted to cry. If this was just talking about it, what would the real thing be like?

"Then what, Sylva?" Malcolm's tone was softened by patience. "Then he'd find you and talk you out of the corner and you'd try again when you calmed down. And if it happened again, he'd find you again. You get the picture. That's the worst-case scenario. Does it sound doable?"

"It sounds humiliating."

"You can survive humiliation. And we both know Harrison will go through that scenario a hundred times for you."

"He'd do it for anyone." While they practiced, Malcolm was relaxed and easygoing, reading her readiness like a master.

"He might, but I've never seen it." He shrugged. "Harrison plays the bad guy in our workshops. Attendees are already half pissing themselves when he walks in, so it gives them a feeling of reality when he's the aggressor."

"But he's a natural."

"Yep. He also has a resting bastard face, so he works that angle." She giggled and he shot her a curious look. "You two seem to be getting along well. Taking a lot of walks together."

"I like his stories."

Malcolm's brows shot up, his brown eyes filled with disbelief. "He's telling stories?"

She nodded. "You know, like your drag racing and how you got mad at him and dug up your mother's roses and blamed him. I'm sure he's told you what we talk about." Now that the environment wasn't as tense, the twins overlapped their schedules so they weren't just two shifters crossing paths twice a day.

Malcolm's jaw dropped. He snapped it closed. "No. He hasn't."

She didn't know what to say. Harrison didn't talk to Malcolm about them? Didn't the twins share *everything*? The urge to ruminate over the finding was too strong. She changed the subject.

"Mind turning around while I shift? I'm still getting used to shifting around others."

Malcolm's eyes narrowed before he turned his back to her. She wasn't the only one who wanted to know more about Harrison's reticence.

CHAPTER 8

Harrison finished the tale of when he'd pretended to be Malcolm in elementary school and gotten yelled at by his sister's friends for changing the height on their bike seats. They were on another walk and were almost to the same clearing as the first night they'd opened up to each other.

Sylva's laughter rang around him like Christmas bells. He grinned and her laughter stopped.

A soft gasp came from her.

He spun around. "Is something wrong?" He didn't sense any danger.

A flush crept up her cheeks. "No, sorry. You smiled."

"And?"

"You don't ever do it," she said and he shot her a questioning look. "Never once since I've known you. I mean, when I've seen you. You know, when you're at the Synod and stuff."

"Were you watching me?"

"No. Not at all." But he could smell her embarrassment. "You're hard not to notice."

"And what did you notice?" He was teasing her and it felt natural.

The look in her eyes turned calculating. "That you're hotter than your brother."

His eyes went wide and he choked out a laugh. No one thought he was the better-looking twin. "We look the same."

"You're taller and your face is more angular."

She was right. But nobody could tell with his beard. "I'm barely a centimeter taller and it depends on who's measuring. We're even when it's Malcolm doing the measuring."

She chuckled. His sense of humor had blossomed in the last few days, but making her laugh had become addictive. She hadn't done nearly enough of it in her life and he aimed to correct that.

"Don't tell him." She was still smiling.

"Definitely not about being hotter. He'd never recover." Harrison would be the one who couldn't get over it. His mind chewed over her confession.

Fuck friendship, he wanted so much more with her.

They passed through the clearing to head back to the cabin. More practice was on the agenda. He'd been so impressed with her progress, he couldn't wait to find out how she fought as her wolf.

She took the lead on the way home, pointing out interesting areas along the way. The spot where she'd found a den of skunks. A mama and three babies, long gone by now. The place where she harvested some mushrooms every year. And the—

He caught a different scent. It smelled like the big cat, Nala. Yet, not exactly. Something was off.

He snaked his hand around her elbow. She stiffened and looked at him like she was wondering if this was part of her training—a surprise attack. He'd never lose her trust that way. She must've read that from his face and she dropped into a defensive crouch.

"I think it's Nala." But from her tone, like him, she detected a difference.

"Something's wrong with your cat. Are there any other mountain lions around?" She would've mentioned it, but he had to ask.

"Not any that smell like her."

Untucking his shirt from his pants, he debated what to do. There was no wind within the trees and it was difficult to detect which direction Nala was coming from. All he knew was that the hairs on the back of his neck were standing up. She was coming for them.

"Do we shift?" Sylva asked. "I can communicate with her better as a wolf."

"Yes." He shed his clothing in seconds and shifted, sweeping around to scent the air.

He sensed Sylva finish her shift. She might be able to communicate with animals using body language, but he couldn't. He would know what Sylva learned if he could mind-speak with her, but he didn't do that with anyone. *Get out of my head, Gloria. Quit interfering with my search.*

No, he couldn't do that again. He'd have to figure out another way.

Nala's scent was growing stronger, and the sour taint on it didn't bode well.

Sylva whined. He glanced at her, but she wasn't looking at him. Her keen gaze was riveted to the trees. The cat. As a human, even with heightened shifter hearing, he wouldn't have heard her approach. She was death on four paws. And she was charging straight for them.

He didn't have time to contemplate what was wrong with her. His one job was to protect Sylva.

Shifters were larger than regular wolves. He was still

bigger than Nala, but she was 130 pounds of agile muscle and her fighting instinct was just as deadly as his.

They met in a clash of claws and fangs. There was no circling to gain the best advantage, no sizing up the opposition. It was how he'd imagine fighting a rabid animal would be like; the higher-thinking part of their brain was shut off and they were just sick and acting on instincts.

Sharp teeth snapped at his neck as she twisted to get a part of him between her powerful jaws. He flipped and rolled, dislodging her, but when he whipped around, she wasn't where he'd expected.

Shit. Nala charged Sylva. The black wolf shimmied to the side, her fangs bared, a warning growl clear in the night. But Nala didn't slow. He sprinted after her, using his powerful haunches to gain speed. The cat was fast, but Sylva evaded her grip long enough for him to pounce.

He caught the cat between his powerful claws and sank his teeth into her thick neck. She snarled and twisted, but he only clamped harder. This shouldn't be so easy. It was like the cat was already fatigued. How long had she been hunting Sylva?

Warm blood filled his mouth. No part of him enjoyed the taste. The coppery tint did nothing to satisfy the hunter in him. Whatever had happened to this cat, it was tragic.

Nala staggered and sank to the ground. He didn't let up. She was too much of a threat to release. The risk was too high. Letting her go wasn't an option.

He sensed a change in the air.

"Harrison, stop." Sylva had shifted back.

The risk was too great. The cat was still fighting against him.

"Harrison. Stop."

Hands pushed at him, but he kept his pressure on the cat. The weakening of her heartbeat told him he wasn't done with this job yet. Somehow she'd been weaponized against them.

"*Stop*. You'll kill her!"

The distress in Sylva's voice was enough to get through to him. He loosened his hold, but as soon as he did, Nala bucked and squirmed for Sylva.

He could tell Sylva what was going on if he could mind-speak with her. The idea made him want to vomit. If he invited her in, would he have to kick her out one day?

An arm snaked around his neck and breasts pressed into his back. She tightened her grip until it forced his jaws to loosen. What the hell was she doing? The cat was going to keep attacking her until its dying breath.

His air was getting cut off. He jerked his teeth from Nala's neck, not realizing how close Sylva still was. He head-butted her. She cried out and released him. When he swung around to see if she was all right, the sight broke his heart.

Sylva scrambled backward until her back hit the trunk of a tree. She was dirty, her knees were skinned, and her torso was covered in blood. He was certain it wasn't hers, and probably not his. The blood was her cat friend's. The one she'd been begging him not to kill.

It was the look in Sylva's eyes that shattered him. When his head had connected with hers, he'd set back all the progress they'd made. And he'd been so careful working with her. Ignoring the cat, he shifted back to his human form. Holding his hands up, he tried to comfort her. "Sylva, it's just me."

She refused to look at him, her watery gaze clued to the prone cat. "D-don't kill her."

"She's rabid. She needs to be put down."

"She's being controlled. That sour smell? I've smelled it before. It's one of Roman's brothers."

He sensed his twin before Sylva did. "Malcolm's coming."

Malcolm came into view, barefoot and wearing jeans. Sylva relaxed. She pressed her fingers against her temples and dragged in a deep breath, then let it out slower.

Malcolm gave him the typical *what did you do?* look. "I got up for some water and smelled blood."

"The cat was trying to kill us," he said as if that was all the explanation he needed. It didn't feel like nearly enough.

"He was going to kill her." Sylva was glaring at him, her arms hugged across her chest and her legs folded to cover herself. He could beat himself for scaring her.

Malcolm went over to the mountain lion. She was still alive, but she'd lost a lot of blood. "She smells weird."

"One of the brothers." He hated seeing what he'd done to the cat, and to Sylva. "Some form of animal mind control."

Malcolm looked at both him and Sylva like the tension between them was visible. "Why don't you two get dressed? I'll walk back with Sylva, and you can carry the cat."

"Her name is Nala." Sylva's voice sounded stronger. Malcolm's presence soothed her. "We're not killing her."

Malcolm shook his head as if that was the worst idea in the world. "Absolutely not. We need to get her out from under shifter control."

He should've sensed it. Instead, he'd overreacted for Sylva's sake and turned into her worst nightmare.

NALA WAS STILL unconscious on the floor of the garage. When they'd returned before dawn, it was the only place the three of them had thought could contain the big cat—if she healed from her injuries. The twins had discussed building a cage but she'd vetoed their idea. The cat wouldn't have much energy for a while and when she did, she was free to go.

Sylva just hoped she'd be able to communicate to Nala that she was safe here.

But was she?

A shifter had gotten close enough to Nala. He'd known she and Nala hung out. The control had been unshakeable until the cat had almost died.

Sylva's heart twisted. She'd brought danger to the creatures of this forest, to the one animal she had some sort of bond with.

She'd dutifully sat on an overturned five-gallon pail through the morning. There was probably an imprint on her ass. Her car was parked outside, looking like a toy next to Malcolm's old pickup. The garage door was open now that the afternoon sun was heating the space to uncomfortable levels. Malcolm patrolled the property.

Harrison had cleaned up and gone to bed. She doubted he was sleeping, but so far, she'd been mostly successful in not thinking about him. When her mind returned to how he'd pinned Nala down, then how sorry he'd looked after he'd shifted, she was conflicted.

What would she have done in his place?

Not killed her friend. But would she have had a choice? She hadn't missed how Nala had continued lunging for her each chance she got. The poor creature.

A water dish was full next to her big head. There was even a pound of hamburger on the floor next to it for when she woke up. The meat should be easy to chew and digest, and about all they could offer since they didn't have access to a veterinarian. Explaining the situation to a nonshifter was out of the question.

Sylva wanted to be here when she woke up. She was the only one who could communicate with her.

Malcolm entered the garage. He put his hands on his hips and studied the mountain lion. "She smells better."

Once they'd removed the cat from the forest and she'd been unconscious long enough, the taint of shifter control had faded. Nala would wake up in pain and terrified. It was still a dangerous situation, but it was the least Sylva could do. Short of getting her head gnawed off, which was what Nala probably had been driven to do, Sylva would survive. Any other injuries Nala could inflict, Sylva could heal from.

"She hasn't moved." Her voice cracked.

Malcolm turned over another bucket and sat next to her, resting his elbows on his knees. "She'll wake up. I'm sure it's the mind control and not the injuries that taxed her."

The injuries. Her own goose egg on her forehead had faded hours ago. The head butt had been an accident, but her mind hadn't understood that at the time.

All that training and she still jumped when a situation brought back memories. What had happened out there in the woods was nothing like her past, but she wasn't going to fool herself. Being around a strong male who acted violently, necessary or not, was a hard obstacle for her to get over.

She should explain that to Harrison, but she couldn't leave her friend's side.

The image of Nala charging at her played through her mind. The cat hadn't stalked her, she hadn't toyed with her, and she hadn't hesitated. She'd been unstoppable.

She copied the way Malcolm was sitting. Her stomach rumbled.

"Harrison made lunch," Malcolm said quietly.

She didn't respond.

"You should eat." Malcolm looked at her from the corner of his eye.

He wasn't pushy but she sensed he wasn't going to let up about her getting fuel—or talking to his brother. "I'm not ready."

"I won't pretend to understand. But my job is to keep you safe and that's a lot harder when you don't trust us."

"I trust you." A slow exhale seeped out of her. She wanted to leave it at that, but she couldn't. Malcolm was worried about her. He cared for his brother more. When she'd been hovering over Nala, Malcolm had tended to Harrison's wounds. "Until Nala wakes up, I just can't think about anything else."

"She means a lot to you."

"He was going to kill her." Dammit, she hated sounding weak.

"She wasn't going to stop," he said softly.

She dropped her hands and rose. Pacing back and forth the short width of her garage, she tried to explain. "I don't make friends, okay? No friends, no family, and my coworkers don't really enjoy my company. It's not like pets are naturally attracted to shifters. It gets lonely out here."

He rubbed his hands over his face. "Will she let us protect her, too?"

"I doubt it. She's a wild animal." And after Harrison, she'd never trust the twins. She might never trust Sylva again. Sorrow hung over her like a dark cloud.

He sighed like he could read her mind. "I'll keep patrolling. We suspected they were out there and now we know."

She'd gotten too complacent, too smug about how the Raymores' scare tactics were just giving her time to learn how to fight them. "I wish I'd known what their abilities were. They were all so secretive." Another control tactic. Her mate had also been discreet.

"It's a hell of an ability." His eyes darkened when he looked at the prone cat. Sylva caught herself before she bared a fang. She might be a little overprotective. "Either one strong brother, or two that can work together to amplify an ability."

What a terrible thought. They could attack her from farther away.

Malcolm left her alone. She crossed to Nala and squatted. Would she heal? Was this endeavor to save her hopeless? When Sylva had first stitched and bandaged her wounds, Nala had soaked through two sets of bandages. This round was still clean. A good sign?

The mountain lion's heartbeat was faint but steadier than it had been earlier.

A shadow blocked the sun. Sylva twisted around.

Harrison.

He was in the garage, but hanging close to the doors. In one hand was a clean set of rags, and a bowl of something steamed from the other. She sniffed. Bone marrow broth.

"I found a bone in the freezer and boiled it up for her." He sounded as concerned as she was.

Bone marrow broth. The soup would be even better than hamburger meat for Nala if they could get it in her.

He stooped and set his stuff down.

"I'm not afraid of you." She bit the inside of her cheek. She sounded scared and defensive. "I'm not afraid."

"It's okay if you are."

She chuffed. "You and Malcolm can quit treating me like I'm fragile at any time."

"Sylva…"

She jumped up and stomped toward him. "I understand, too. I'm lonely and pathetic. You two feel sorry for me. You're always worried about scaring me. You saved my life and now you have to tiptoe around me because you're worried about my fragile state. I hate it. And if you keep treating me like this, I'll hate you, too."

She gasped and pressed two fingers to her lips. What had

come out of her mouth? None of it made sense. Or it made perfect sense. Her mind was a mess.

And judging by his perplexed expression, he thought so, too.

She released a frustrated growl, grabbed his shirt, and planted her lips on his.

He stiffened under her grip but made no move to push her away. His hands stayed by his side and his lips didn't yield under hers. But this wasn't a romantic kiss. It shocked her mind into screaming *What are you doing?* and she had to answer.

What was she doing?

As she pulled away, she puzzled over the kiss. She and Harrison had surmounted a big obstacle in the days before the attack, and they'd been growing even closer.

Now, her traumatized mind wanted to be terrified of him. It wanted to blame him for the dying cat on her garage floor. And that broke her heart.

What was worse? Never having anything to lose, or gaining it and then losing it?

She licked her lips and forced herself to look into his dark eyes. "I'm sorry for such a drastic move. I don't hate you, of course."

"You didn't claim to." His shoulders loosened but he was far from relaxed. "I didn't take it that way." She cocked her head. "Okay, maybe a little. But logically I knew—"

"It's the logical part we need to hang on to." She tapped her forehead. "This isn't making the most sense right now. I'm trying to be the new me."

"You can't be the new you without the old you. That female survived a lot. She was a survivor. A fighter."

"I didn't… Without my mother…"

He cocked his head. "What did your mother actually do?"

"It was her idea," Sylva whispered. "The gun. We were

convinced it was the only way to free myself. But I couldn't do it."

Harrison's incredulous face was frozen while he processed what she'd said. "Your *mother* shot your mate?"

Shame oozed from all her pores. It was hard to admit, but she trusted him. She nodded. "I couldn't do it. John Todd was right. I was cowardly."

"Your mate went out of his way to make sure it was the only way for you to free yourself. And if he'd have thought you could do something like that, he would've taken that away, too."

She hadn't thought about it like that. "How do you always know the right thing to say? Do you have a lot of experience with trauma victims?"

Color leached from his face. "No. My, um, my mate had similar concerns and I tried to make her feel better. I tried."

There was so much about him and this mysterious mate he'd lost that she wanted to know about. She was about to ask when his gaze darted to Nala.

Sylva spun and rushed to the cat's side. Had she moved?

The cat's massive paws twitched, then her whiskers. Her eyes blinked open halfway, the inner eyelid still in place. More twitching, a little blinking.

Harrison backed away. "She'll react better if I'm not around, but I won't be far."

Good. She never wanted him far away.

CHAPTER 9

*H*arrison looked out the window as he finished the dishes. Malcolm was behind him and he could sense all the questions his brother was dying to ask.

What happened in the garage?

Seriously, what happened?

All Malcolm said was "You don't look like a pound puppy anymore."

"I didn't look like one before, jackass."

It was only seven p.m. They'd decided to alternate their shift changes an hour in either direction to keep it unpredictable, but Harrison had been up for hours.

"You sure you don't need more sleep?" Malcolm asked.

"I'm fine." He couldn't sleep. After that weird kiss, he definitely wouldn't get a second of shut-eye.

Her lips had been so soft. And the way her cherry-blossom scent had wrapped around him, he couldn't get it out of his head.

As awkward and perfunctory as it'd been, the badly timed kiss had blown his mind. And he couldn't quit thinking about it. After what had happened with Nala, he'd thought he was not only back to square one with Sylva, but even farther behind. She had so few close connections in her life and he'd nearly killed one of them.

"How's Nala?" Malcolm asked.

"Sylva managed to get some broth into her."

"Good call."

It was the least he could do. He hadn't wanted to kill her and regretted that so much force had been necessary.

"She scared?" Malcolm asked.

"She's too weak to feel much. I wish there was more online, but rehabbing mountain lions doesn't seem to be recommended for the average person." Though they weren't average, and Sylva was determined. They could've called a vet, but he didn't trust the brothers not to get to Nala in someone else's custody. "She'll heal. She's survived this long living in shifter territory."

"Demke couldn't find any info on the Raymores. They've been able to slip through the gaps, keeping their colony shit to themselves and not drawing attention. But he did find that Raymores often mate within the colony, and pretty young, too."

"You and I met our mates young."

Malcolm didn't have to say *Look how that turned out*. He glanced toward the door, making sure Sylva was still outside. "It's unusual, but not for them. I mean, like *every* Raymore finds their true mate young. It's like they breed their own mates."

"Maybe it's fate because they're so isolated." That was a lame guess. Demke's findings were more than odd. "But she said they were true mates."

"I call shenanigans."

He draped his rag over the faucet, taking his time to keep

from ripping it to shreds. "You think they tampered with our nature and are *creating* true mates?"

"I think it's possible. We have the ability to cast wards to protect our Guardian headquarters from being discovered by humans. You've heard Demetrius's reports, demons and underworld shit. Why not this, too?"

Why not indeed. "Get some sleep. I'll check on Sylva and go patrol."

Malcolm didn't move. "What happened in the garage?"

"Couldn't help yourself, could you?"

Malcolm scowled, reminding him of when they were five and Malcolm refused to admit where he'd hidden the new toy truck they were supposed to share.

"We talked. We're fine."

"She's not fine and neither are you."

No, he wasn't. "It's not your business."

"Your issues with Gloria weren't my business. You and Sylva are."

"What the fuck does Gloria have to do with any of this?" Couldn't Malcolm quit being so perceptive for once?

"She was scared of you, too."

"Sylva's not scared of me. Not anymore." She wouldn't have kissed him if she were. But then, Gloria had, pretending to be strong.

"She was cowering from you less than twenty-four hours ago. I'm just trying to keep you from going off the deep end again. I don't want another Gloria."

"Sylva's not Gloria, and Sylva and I are just friends." And he had not gone off the deep end.

"Sylva might not be Gloria, but I've never seen you this way around someone. Except Gloria, and she couldn't handle you. There are a lot of parallels."

"None of which were what got Gloria killed." And there were a lot of differences. Sylva owned her leadership position, and she wanted to defend herself and not rely on Harrison to do it.

Gloria should've been one of the strongest in the pack. Her parents were colony leaders and she could've been their uncontested heir. But instead of learning to use her strength, she'd relied on her beauty and people-pleasing skills. She could have been killed in a fight for power and she'd known it.

She'd loved and hated that Harrison's family gave zero fucks when it came to what others thought of them and they had the brawn to back it up. Looking to him to fight her battles had been her strategy.

Then one day, he hadn't been around to protect her. She'd tried to contact him and he'd ignored her.

Apparently, Malcolm wasn't done with the subject. "I know full well what—*who*—killed your mate. Which is why I need you to keep being the Harrison you've been for years. Father isn't our leader any longer. He can't save your ass if something happens to Sylva and you go on a rampage."

Those shifters had deserved to die. They'd seeded fear and then toyed with Gloria like she was the feeder kitten in a dog fight. But he was done with this subject. "Want to talk about mates? Let's discuss yours and how happy she is with another male. How has that changed you?"

Malcolm squeezed the bridge of his nose. "Harrison…"

The front door clicked open. They hadn't been shouting, but their voices had been raised and shifters had excellent hearing. How much had Sylva heard? He didn't want her to know the story. As much as he hated to admit Malcolm was right, there were too many parallels and Sylva didn't need to hear an unhappy ending.

"I'm going on patrol." He spun on his heel, and taking the coward's route, he kept his head down as he whisked out the door. His boots had barely touched the dirt before he was stripping down and shifting. But as he trotted to the edge of the trees, he had the feeling that he was running off again on someone who needed him.

SYLVA SHIFTED HER POSITION. She stood post over Nala in her wolf form so that when the cat woke up, she'd be ready.

It had been twenty-four hours since the attack. Nala had woken up, lapped some broth, and slept. She'd kept that routine into the night, but she'd also started moving her limbs and adjusting her body. In another day, she might get up and walk around.

Before she shifted, she'd washed Nala's tawny coat, removing blood and grit from the fight. After receiving a tense smile and a goodnight from Malcolm after the obvious fight with Harrison, she'd brought out a fresh batch of broth.

The bits of angry words she'd heard had filled in part of the story.

She thought back to Harrison when she'd first been broken out of prison and then thrust into serving on the Synod. He'd been competent, doing his job and ignoring her. Hadn't that made her feel like nothing had changed. Another male who thought she was merely a weak shifter. And sons of a former member of the Lycan Council to boot, the leaders who had enabled shifters like the Raymores to abuse their power. That had been the biggest strike against them. So she'd guarded herself against them.

But their father had gladly walked away from his leadership position. From what she understood, he'd been phoning in most of his duties anyway. Did the twins have anything to do with him? Or their mother?

She mulled over the memory of her own parents. Roman had effectively cut her off, restricting and shortening visits until she had to beg for weeks. After Mother helped her kill him, they hadn't seen each other again. Sylva couldn't bring herself to check on her. Mother might've gotten her access to the gun and the bullets, but she'd also let her own daughter get mated off like a not-so-prized horse.

Soft steps caught her ear. Harrison's heady scent teased her nose. He smelled like sweat, fresh air, and pine trees—all male. It should be enough to send her running, but she wanted to breathe harder, to suck it all in.

Harrison's scent was so unlike her mate's. There was no deception, no lingering smells of others' pain, and definitely not the scent of the brothers. Always the brothers. John Todd, Rafe, and Clayton had been a constant in her life. That they hadn't been living under the same roof as her was a shock. But Roman wouldn't have allowed it. He had better control living on his own with a mate he could lord over them.

Harrison was hovering outside the open garage door. She couldn't call out and tell him it was okay to come inside. Mind-speak, maybe, but she hadn't made that much progress. Once she'd gotten Roman's ugly, hurtful voice out of her head, she'd had no interest in inviting another back in.

He finally entered the garage, still in wolf form, and settled on his haunches next to her. They both watched the cat's chest rise and fall.

If he were in his human form, she could imagine what he'd say. *She's doing better.*

And she'd tell him, *Yes, she drank the whole bowl of broth.* She might even nervously chatter and say, *I got another bowl, but with the bugs, I had to put a cloth over it. She can probably still smell what's inside and get to it if I'm not here.*

At that, he'd reply, *You should get some rest.*

And she'd agree, but simply shrug as much as her wolf

would allow and they'd sit in silence before she offered, *I can't leave her until I know that she knows she's safe here.*

And he'd go, *I know.*

He got on all fours and padded out. She swore the thought *I'll be right outside* hung on the air.

CHAPTER 10

*H*arrison was pulling his jeans on when soft footsteps broke through his thoughts.

"Was it my imagination," tentative interest clung to her words, "or did we have some odd kind of mental conversation?"

He hadn't yet pulled on his boots or his shirt, and he wished for an entire suit of armor to keep from answering her question. Or to help hide his body stirring at the sight of her curvy silhouette outlined in the moonlight. It shouldn't be that clear, the moon was only half full, but there were no clouds and it was like the stars cast their light just for her.

She'd pulled her cream robe back on and her arms were crossed in front of her, but not like when she was confronting an angry petitioner at the Synod. Yet she wasn't hugging herself either, like when she'd been curled up in her cellar.

She was embracing her strength.

"I don't mind-speak." He didn't mean to sound so abrupt. Dropping his shoulders, he expected her to scurry away with rightfully hurt feelings.

"No, I know. I mean, I get it. I don't either." Her smile was hesitant. "Probably for different reasons."

"He hurt you with his thoughts."

She pushed a lock of hair behind her ear and tucked her hand back into the fold of her other arm. "Not as often as you might expect. But his words were always on replay. He knew exactly what to say so he didn't have to keep repeating himself."

She'd shared so much. Did she realize she was speaking about her past in a more confident tone and with less apprehension? The female cowering in that prison cell years ago wouldn't have been able to. Her act was no longer a show.

"I was gone." He could kick himself but he couldn't quit talking. "Gloria didn't want me to go, but she couldn't forbid me to. We were so young, I thought we had forever. And she was in my head." *Please come back to me, Harrison. I need you.* "Always in my head. We weren't finding Camille, and Gloria was begging me to return, and I snapped. I told her to get out of my head and suck it up until I got home."

She drifted closer. "Then they got to her."

Why had he opened his big mouth? Reliving his biggest regret in front of Sylva was the perfect nightmare. "*They* were a rival pack. We all knew they'd challenge her for leadership, but her parents were still alive. She had nothing to worry about. But while I was gone, there was a fire. Her parents survived. Then her mother nearly died from silver poisoning. Gloria was so scared. She tried to contact me when—I ignored her." He hung his head. Finding Camille had consumed him. "I should've gone back. She was sweet and threatened no one as the heir."

"Let me guess. They weren't worried about her until they learned you were her true mate. It'd be harder to challenge her when you could do the same and take the colony back."

Gloria's guileless, soft brown eyes and her innocent smile

swam in his head. He hadn't opened his mind to anyone since then. "Then I was gone and she was as vulnerable as she'd ever been."

"When her parents didn't die, they went for her."

Air whooshed out of him, deflating him until he sank to the ground. "And I was miles away."

She sat next to him, sinking effortlessly to her butt and curling her legs next to her. She still hugged her robe to herself. "You felt her death." He could hug her sympathy to him, use it to mop up the helpless feelings warring inside of him.

"I knew the moment her heart quit beating. I tore through the colony, ripping apart the three shifters involved." He stretched his legs out and propped his arms behind him. Dropping his head back, he gazed at the moon. "They lured her out to the trees, and when she was alone…"

He didn't see the moon anymore. The loss of the connection, the way it had shattered in a second and was gone. If he'd properly mated Gloria, he would've died when she had. He wouldn't have been one of those empty mates who could keep going.

He'd done everything for her. He'd waited for her, abstaining until she was ready, but when she'd begged him to come to her, he'd shut her out.

Sylva laid her hand on his arm. He didn't snap his arm away—his typical reaction to touch. Instead, he leaned into the comfort of her warmth. Her small hand had rendered him unable to think.

It was bliss.

For once, he wasn't plagued with everything he'd done wrong. The memory of Gloria's sweet, innocent smile didn't fill him with guilt, but pleasant recollection.

More of his tragic story refused to be contained. "Malcolm thought our connection made her more insecure."

"That's too bad."

Not the comment he'd been expecting. "What do you mean?"

She withdrew her hand. It was all he could do to keep his planted in the grass and not reach for it. "I was just thinking earlier about the way you and Malcolm are. It's how Roman and his brothers should've been."

"It's a twin thing."

"Maybe," she murmured. "But your closeness should be celebrated. You protect each other, and together, your ability to do good for your kind is amplified. I'm glad you were the one Demke called."

Leaving Sylva's well-being in someone else's care sounded ridiculous. Damn right, Demke had called him. He met her violet gaze, seeing the moonlight shine in her eyes. "Me, too."

He shifted so smoothly, neither one of them had time to react. He was on his hip, leaning into her, his mouth poised over hers.

Did she want this? Did he? He wasn't the romantic type. He didn't kiss. He didn't snuggle. He didn't share any of himself with anyone. He shouldn't get to experience this when he'd squandered his chance.

What was he thinking?

He was about to retreat when Sylva moved forward, her lips brushing his. Her blossom scent closed around him and he pressed his lips to hers.

Two kisses now and this female had him wound up in knots.

He should stop. This wasn't sex. Sex was useful, practical. It was a way to use up extra energy and hormones and pheromones and whatever the hell had his dick insisting he get laid. Kissing was so much more than that.

Her breath wafted over his cheek, so warm, so soft, just

like her. He held himself tight, fighting the temptation to push her back onto the grass and yank open her robe, see how luscious those breasts of hers really were.

But he was already leaning into her until she was unfolding beneath him. If they kept going like this, she'd be under him.

She'd be under him in nothing but a robe held together by a narrow strip of cloth.

A low growl escaped him. Need pounded through his blood, rushing to his cock until the clasp of his pants dug into his flesh.

A faint growl broke through the crickets chirping.

Sylva lunged upward, shoving him off with enough force to send him tumbling onto his ass.

"Nala!" She jumped up, shed her robe, and shifted as she ran.

He didn't follow right away. Not because of the raging erection he sported or because he was worried he'd frighten the cat.

He was mesmerized by the brief moment of seeing Sylva's ripe butt cheeks flex and bunch as she ran off.

SYLVA FINISHED CLEANING up the garage. Three days after waking, Nala had disappeared into the trees, heading in the direction of her den.

It was shift change and she wanted to be done out here before she had to face Harrison. They were switching later than normal tonight. It gave her the perfect excuse to be settled into her bath without looking like a coward who'd been avoiding him for three days.

As long as she was by the cat, he kept his distance. Nala growled whenever he came near, but the twins didn't trust

Nala enough to stay too far away. Their nightly patrols cast a wide net, enough to ensure Roman's brothers couldn't get close enough to control Nala.

Malcolm leaned against the frame of the open garage door. "I'm worried they'll get to her again. It'd cause you mental anguish."

She hugged the empty water bowl to herself. "She's a wild cat. I can't keep her prisoner."

His look said that yes, they could. It was a gamble. Sylva would stay away from the forest until her troubles were over. Whenever that would be.

Then she'd be back to living alone.

Clutching the plastic water bowl tighter, she scurried inside and ran into a wide chest.

Strong hands circled her arms to keep her from rebounding back. Harrison's scent swamped her now that it wasn't blocked by the door.

"S-sorry." She forced herself to look up at him. Her gaze hit his lips first and her body clenched. For such a strong male, he'd been tender, knowing exactly when she was ready for the next step.

She'd been pressed into the ground with him over her and she'd wanted nothing more than for him to drop his weight on top of her. She'd wanted him between her legs and thrusting.

Hastily stepping back, she mourned the loss of his touch as he let her slip through his fingers. She sidled around him. "Malcolm's outside." Which he'd know.

"Jonathon called."

She finished her trek into the kitchen. The Synod was calling Harrison first more often. She wasn't the only one sensing a change in him. "Is something wrong?"

Harrison appeared at the island. "He said the Synod would like to meet tonight."

Her front door opened and closed. "We're getting low on supplies," Malcolm called. "I say we go."

Harrison didn't take his steady gaze off her. "It could be what they're waiting for."

She was a homebody, but she was also dedicated to her work. Being imprisoned in her own home was getting old. "Then let's do it. We're ready for them. Right?"

The twins exchanged a look she couldn't read but was probably an entire conversation.

Malcolm dipped his head and looked at her. "You should be armed."

She bit the inside of her cheek to keep from refusing. They were talking about arming her and they probably didn't mean that stupid pistol. "Armed with what?"

"Do you think you can remember the knife moves we taught you?" Malcolm asked. "We didn't get much time."

She nodded as she beelined for her room. Being armed didn't mean she'd have to use them. "I'll get dressed."

When she emerged in more official-looking slacks and a silk top, Harrison was waiting for her. He looked the same. Navy T-shirt, blue jeans, and boots. But her belly flipped and ignited a spark that she tried to extinguish.

His gaze swept the length of her body, leaving a brush fire behind wherever it touched. "Are you okay with those clothes getting ruined if we're in a fight?"

She refused to be disappointed that he hadn't been checking her out. "They're just clothes. I can get more."

He held out a holstered knife, hilt pointing toward her. "This is silver-laced steel."

Her hand hovered above the handle. Silver. This knife could kill with nothing but a nick. She wrapped her fingers around it. "You have salt, just in case?"

"In the pickup." He didn't sound irritated that she'd asked.

Salt would be a standard supply for Guardians to neutralize silver toxicity.

Holding the knife, she looked down at herself. "Where should I wear it?" The guys made it hard to tell they were armed. Harrison's shirt was so snug it only showed sinful muscle. He wasn't wearing a knife on his torso. She'd guess in his boots, but she was wearing flats.

He scrutinized her body, narrowing his gaze on her waist. Twisting, he pointed to his lower back. "Right here. Under your shirt. If trouble starts, just flip your shirt up like this." The flash of smooth skin sent a hot flash through her.

She went back to her bedroom to secure it. Lifting her shirt around him wasn't a good idea when she was supposed to be professional and protect herself from an attack. Her lack of focus could get them hurt.

He was still there when she emerged. "Sylva..." His jaw clenched and he looked frustrated at himself. "How are you doing since Nala left?"

Had he wanted to talk about their kiss? She did. But only in a *When can we do it again?* way and that didn't help either of them. Friends didn't make out like they wanted to fuck.

She didn't have any friends, but she knew that much.

"She's safer in the wild. Even with your patrols, they could get to her here."

An engine fired up outside. She started for the door.

"If you feel something off, tell us." Harrison's statement stopped her.

"Of course."

He closed the distance between them. "And if shit goes down, do whatever we say, but take care of yourself first. Don't worry about us."

"Right." She cocked her head. "Are you okay?"

"I...don't want you hurt."

"I don't want you hurt either."

The corner of his mouth hitched up. "And that's why you're more important. Our kind needs you."

"I need you," she whispered.

His mouth claimed hers. She twined her arms around his neck. This was what she'd wanted. She'd been missing it for three days. His touch. His smell surrounding her.

His tongue swept inside her mouth and she greedily opened for him. She hadn't ever kissed like this. She'd tried but Roman hadn't had the patience.

Harrison grasped her waist, careful of the knife at her back. He was always aware of her and how to handle her. She would've bristled at the thought of being handled, but not with him. She appreciated it. She needed it.

A honk startled them apart.

She propped one hand on her hip and stuffed the other through her freshly combed hair. "We can't ignore this."

"You're right. And I don't want to. I thought I did, but I don't want to."

She felt the same. "Let's get tonight over with first."

He gestured for her to go first. As she walked out of the door, he said, "I'm serious, Sylva. Trust us to handle ourselves and watch out for yourself."

CHAPTER 11

I don't like this vibes bounced back and forth between him and his twin. Harrison was posted on the other side of the Synod door. Malcolm paced the antechamber space, occasionally stopping to check out the front door.

"They're not just going to walk in here." It was a sign of his growing bitchiness that he even spoke.

Malcolm stopped and propped a hand on the wall. "Want to tell me why she was so flushed when you guys came out of the house?"

Harrison clenched his jaw. He'd hoped Malcolm hadn't noticed.

"Shit." His brother's hand slipped off the wall as he returned to pacing. "Of all the times…"

"Not here." Too many people with excellent hearing.

"Should the three of us sit and talk this out when we get back?"

"It's none of your business." It felt wrong as soon as he said it. "It won't affect our work."

Malcolm came close, his voice a ragged whisper. "The hell

it won't. Between your history and not knowing how she'll react in an emergency, we're sitting on a Roman candle of—"

"Was that a pun?"

"I'm not joking."

"I didn't say you were."

Malcolm pinned him with an incredulous look. "Are you seriously being obtuse right now?"

Harrison tipped his head back to the wall. "We'll talk about it later." He didn't know what they'd talk about. He and Sylva had tried to be responsible adults but then they kept kissing.

What did he know about this stuff?

That he wanted more. That he didn't deserve more. That it didn't matter when she was near, he wanted more.

Malcolm's concerns were warranted. While he didn't relish trying to figure out what these feelings were between him and Sylva in front of his twin, they had to. For their own safety, but for her safety most of all.

"She should learn how to use firearms." Malcolm's subject change left him reeling. "She doesn't want to, but they'll give her an advantage."

"She'll agree to it."

Malcolm leaned closer, his voice syrupy sweet. "If you ask her, she will."

"Asshole."

Malcolm chuckled and went back to pacing.

A few long minutes had ticked by when the door to the chamber creaked open.

"All done." Sylva's gaze was steady, her head held high. She had donned her Synod personality. Cool and impervious.

Had he once been annoyed by it? It was as sexy as when she walked around in nothing but a robe before she shifted.

He knew the real her, and more importantly, he understood why she acted the way she did. Their people wouldn't follow a quiet and contemplative leader. She didn't use physical force, but she demonstrated strength with her unyielding decisions and work ethic.

Malcolm took point as they walked to the pickup. It was parked in the loop by the entrance. Harrison waited until Sylva was settled into the backseat before he hopped into the front.

"Getting groceries shouldn't be this nerve-racking," Malcolm muttered as he threw the pickup into drive.

The store was uneventful. Malcolm was more successful at looking casual. Sylva kept her Synod persona in place. Harrison glared at everyone and everything.

With groceries safely tucked into the back with Sylva, they hit the highway to her place. Once Malcolm turned off onto the gravel road, he cracked his window.

Different smells filtered in, all of them familiar. Trees, wildlife, the rain that was a few miles off.

As the pickup slowed to turn into the long driveway that wound through the trees to the cottage, Harrison lowered his window, too. Nothing.

Malcolm parked. "It can't be this easy."

No, it couldn't. They'd left the house. Either they'd snuck through the brothers' blind spot or they were missing something.

Harrison sucked in a deep breath at the same time Sylva said, "I smell blood."

A metallic tang stained the air. Malcolm kicked the pickup into gear and gave it enough gas to roll in front of the house. A sharp gasp came from the backseat.

A bloody X was carved into the front door. A red, gooey lump was anchored to the porch boards with a knife.

"That was Roman's hunting knife," Sylva said in a ragged voice. "I'd recognize it anywhere."

"Stay here." Malcolm slipped out and circled the pickup before crossing to the house.

Harrison scanned the trees and kept dragging in lungfuls of air. He registered the blood smell. An animal. Under that was shifter. Two shifters.

Malcolm disappeared into the house. Harrison struggled to stay relaxed and ready as he lost sight of his brother. He couldn't leave Sylva, no matter what happened.

When his twin reemerged, the look on his face told him that it was worse inside. Malcolm lifted his chin toward the yard. He was going to shift and search the property.

"Did he tell you what was wrong?" Fear spiked Sylva's soft scent. He hated the brothers for it.

"Not specifically." She wouldn't be able to go into her house. Whatever message the blood on the door sent, there was more inside.

"It's ruined, isn't it?"

He inclined his head enough for her to see his answer.

"Can we go inside so I can see for myself?"

He wanted to say no, to smuggle her away and help her forget about the three brothers that hated her. But he slipped out and opened her door.

Her nostrils flared in the blood-soaked air. "It's from a cat." A ripple traveled through her body. A full wave of grief. She closed her eyes and inhaled. "But not from Nala.

Not this time. He stayed by her side as they reached the porch. The heart speared to the porch floorboards was larger than a house cat's. It'd be the right size for a mountain lion's.

They couldn't catch Nala again, but they'd lured another cat to them to use against Sylva.

Sylva stared at the dripping red X on her front door. It wouldn't do their anxiety any good to stand out here and wonder how bad it was. He stepped around her and opened the door.

The air inside was thick with blood. Large gouges were carved out of her hardwood floors. One of the brothers must've shifted and clawed whatever he touched.

"Those assholes." Sylva started the walk through her house. Blood stained the carpets, was splattered on the walls, and anything that was made from fabric or wood—which included her entire house—had been altered in some way, and not for the better.

They should've had someone watching the place while they were gone. He and Malcolm should've wired security cameras and alarms during the last week, but they'd respected Sylva's need for discretion and privacy.

It had cost her. It shouldn't have, but it had cost her nearly everything.

She wandered through the house like a zombie, her face registering nothing. Peering into her bedroom, she stiffened and stepped back, her complexion paler than when they'd entered.

He peeked in. A mangled hide was stretched across her bed. A mountain lion. He'd make Rafe and Clayton pay. The room he'd used was destroyed, too, his clothing shredded.

Back in the entry, she pressed her fingers to her forehead. Then with a strangled gasp, she rushed downstairs. He followed.

A cloud of air thick with tangy salt and vinegar enveloped him.

"Bastards," she snarled.

Glass was shattered all over the floor. Pickling juice stained everything. Green juice from cucumbers and beans and red juice from beets mingled on the floor. His nose twitched with the heavy dill smell. Her cellar had been wiped out. Every jar busted. Years of work and hours upon hours of labor, gone.

Her shoulders shook. Without thinking, he crossed to her and closed her in his embrace. A sob shook her.

This was her passion. Playing with her cat friends, tending the earth, and preserving the food she grew was her heart and they'd shredded it. That family continued to take from her and not face any consequences.

He'd make sure they paid. He'd make sure they never bothered Sylva or another shifter again. This time, he wasn't going anywhere.

～

HARRISON'S HUG was the safest place in the world. She was torn between wanting to lean into him and lose herself, and hating herself for needing it so much.

Fury made his skin hot, but he kept it contained. His expression was a mix of thunderclouds and compassion.

The compassion almost did her in. This was all her fault. The attack and the harassment and the animal's death were on Rafe and Clayton, but that they could get here, get to her, was on her.

Damn her pride.

"Cameras would've done no good." The words rumbled against her cheek, which was pressed to his chest. He had sensed the change in her grief and followed her thoughts.

"An alarm system might've stopped them."

"No. They would've ignored it. We were miles away."

"Someone could've been stationed here, protecting the house." She shook her head as she said it, disagreeing with herself. "But I couldn't ask someone to put themselves in harm's way to protect me."

"Yes, you could."

"I have no right."

"You're one of our leaders. You're important to the people."

She let out a scornful laugh. "They wouldn't care if it was me or another shifter up there. They trust Demke because he's faithfully led them for years and was the only voice to support them during the Lycan Council's time." She winced, realized what she'd said. "I mean, I'm sure your father—"

"Ignored what didn't fit his own agenda even if it was best for the people. You're right about Demke."

She relaxed, the initial shock of the night wearing off. She released herself from his embrace. "I should get started cleaning."

"I'll help until Malcolm comes back. Then we'll decide how to do this."

Upstairs, she dug out mop pails, then went about piling rags and rubber gloves and sponges on the counter. Her clothes were rumpled and bloodstained just from walking through the house, but it didn't slow her down. They were probably in better shape than anything else she owned.

Filling a bucket with soapy water, she headed for his room.

"Where are you going?" Harrison asked. Had he expected her to start on her room first?

There was a dead animal on her bed. Her intentions should be altruistic, but she didn't want to face her bedroom. "You and Malcolm need a place to rest. I'll do your rooms first, then work my way around the house."

"I'll see to the carcass."

Her mouth tightened. "Thank you," she said quietly and disappeared into his room. She'd been telling him that a lot lately.

They worked for an hour before Malcolm came back, his footsteps above her head were light for such a big male. Sylva had finished cleaning what she could of the blood stains from Harrison's bedroom and was downstairs in Malcolm's.

Harrison had opened all the windows and buried the dead cat with its heart. For the last half hour, he'd been remaking her bed and sifting through clothing, deciding what could get washed and what needed to be thrown away.

Most of it would get tossed. It had been pissed on, the smell more pungent than all the pickling juice spilled in the basement. She went upstairs, listening to the twins' conversation.

"They're long gone, but I doubt they're far away," Malcolm said. His entrance brought in a clean pine scent. She'd gotten used to the blood, but a fresh smell was welcome.

"They're cowards," Harrison replied.

"That, I agree with. But cowards can be the dirtiest fighters."

"She won't be able to sleep in here. They marked it like animals. I'd say we should go to a hotel tonight, but they'd probably just come back and burn it down."

Neither of them had noticed her. "I've slept in worse."

Both of their sharp gazes pinned her. How could they both look so rugged and handsome while she was a rumpled, smelly, tired female? Her silky hair was tied back with a scrap from a rag, and a half-billed bucket of murky brown water hung in one hand.

Harrison rose. "You don't need to sleep in worse. Take my bedroom. I'll sleep on the couch."

"The springs are exposed on the couch." It'd be the base of a big bonfire in the morning.

"Then Malcolm and I will share downstairs. We never sleep at the same time anyway."

"Sylva." Malcolm frowned at the bucket in her hand. "I'm

really sorry to heap more bad news on today, but...your gardens have been dug up."

He might as well have shoved a knife hilt deep in her chest. The destruction of her canned goods was equal to hours of her life thrown away like they didn't matter. But her gardens had been alive, thriving, growing.

And now they were gone.

Tears gathered in her eyes but she refused to let them spill. "Thank you for telling me."

"Let's call it for the night." Malcolm pushed open the bathroom door. It was surprisingly untouched, but that made sense. There wasn't enough fabric to destroy and it'd take too long and expend too much energy to damage ceramic and porcelain. "I'm gonna take a shower and grab a few hours."

She was left facing Harrison as he stood in the middle of the wreckage of her room.

Pointing to the bed with a stain of blood across its white mattress, she said, "Tomorrow morning, we can start burning stuff."

"Get some rest, Sylva. We'll figure the rest out later."

He'd be on duty the rest of the night, which was only a few hours before dawn. The bucket still needed to be dumped and she had to find clean clothing that was in good enough shape to cover her body. "I need to get some fresh air." And see all of her hard work gone to waste.

She emptied and rinsed her bucket and rags. Harrison waited at the door for her.

Outside, she heaved a breath full of night air. The taint of blood, while still clinging to her porch, was less concentrated. Making the trek to her gardens took as much effort as wading through hip-deep mud.

It was like Malcolm had said. The soil looked like a pack of wild dogs with a digging addiction had swept through, leaving nothing but the stench of urine and straggly roots pointing toward the sky. She wouldn't be able to save any produce. What hadn't been outright ruined from digging had been pissed on. Had the brothers been saving their urine just for this?

Standing here, witnessing the destruction of her property, didn't fill her with the despair that had pounded her inside the house. This was her home. She'd earned it. She'd worked for it. Her time and her money were sunk into this place, and a couple of overgrown bullies with a god complex were not scaring her off. "They're not driving me from my home."

"Good."

Energy stirred inside of her. It'd been a week filled with nursing Nala back to health, now capped with trying to rescue her home. She strode up and down the length of her garden. "They aren't going to make me feel weak again."

He didn't reply. She liked that about him. He didn't feel the need to talk over her, or roll his eyes at her emotions, or destroy her stuff.

She spun and stomped back. "They don't own me. They never did." Reaching the edge of the garden, she pivoted again. "I'm not weak and I'm not owned." Restlessness churned under her skin until she was afraid she'd burst. She couldn't run the forest because of them.

And what happened if she could? She'd hide her body again? Shifters embraced their form, especially their nudity. They embraced their sexuality. And wouldn't that be a good way to burn off her energy? To take back her life?

She veered off course to stop in front of Harrison. A little voice in her head was shouting in alarm, but she talked over that voice like Roman used to do to her.

"Have sex with me."

CHAPTER 12

Those words did not go with the night he'd had. He'd watched her hold in tears. He'd been with her as they sifted through the ravaged remains of her home. And she wanted to have sex?

But there was more there. Her eyes were reflective, like a predator's. Her pulse was racing, her breathing increased. She was vibrant. Filled with vitality. In her eyes was the determination to reclaim herself as she'd saved her possessions.

A tendril of disappointment curled inside him. She wanted him for sex, to use him to reclaim the wild creature she was never allowed to be.

A stronger male than him would say no. A male who was true to himself would back off until the female he was falling for wanted to be with him just because it was him.

But it wasn't as if he hadn't let females use him for orgasms for years. He was good at it, to the point of being mechanical.

Sylva's need was different from the other females he'd been with. He could serve her as well in this as he had in protecting her the last couple of weeks. She trusted him with her safety, and he would prove she could trust him with this, too.

The fact that she'd be the first partner he hadn't shared with his twin wasn't lost on him. He wouldn't explore that further, just like he wouldn't explore the gnawing sense that it wasn't enough, that thinking of himself as nothing but a stepping stone on her path to a better life *hurt*.

Yeah, he didn't need to look into those feelings.

She was still looking at him for an answer. To give her one, he peeled his shirt off.

Her scent bloomed around him. Arousal. Her gaze brushed over his body, stopping at his chest, dipping down to his stomach, then farther to where his growing erection pushed against his pants.

Taking his time, he undid the clasp. Usually he undressed as Malcolm was getting busy. Having a partner's attention solely on him was a foreign sensation.

Don't read into it. She just wanted sex like the rest. She didn't ask for cuddling or promises, and if circumstances were different, she probably wouldn't even ask for a date. There was no kissing.

Rolling his jeans down freed his dick. Her delicate inhale drew his attention. Her appreciative gaze was on his jutting manhood. A trace of apprehension laced her scent.

How bad of a setback would it be for her if she stopped? Her mate had probably mounted her and left when he was done. Only she knew how much control she'd had in sex, but he guessed it wasn't much.

"You're in charge." As he said it, he had an idea. Stepping out of his boots and clothing, he said, "I'm yours to explore tonight."

Her startled gaze flew to his, then trailed down his body. "I don't know what to do."

"Whatever you want." He'd prefer to be indoors and in a bed, but if he had to get a little dirt up his ass to give her privacy, so be it.

She took a step closer. "I want..." Another step. "To touch you."

"Whatever you want." Wasn't that how he'd gotten into this position? It wasn't about what he secretly wished for in his life. This was about helping her. Protecting her.

She came close enough to reach her hand out. Her fingers landed on his chest. "You're beautiful."

A part of him that he hadn't known existed sparked to life. "Don't tell Malcolm you said that," he rumbled.

She smiled and trailed her fingers down until they floated over his erection. His breath hitched. A decision crossed over her face a second before she closed her hand around him.

He bucked his hips and she loosened her grip. Catching her hand in his, he gritted through clenched teeth. "That wasn't a sign to quit."

"It feels good?"

So good it threatened to drive him to his knees. "Yes."

Her soft chuckle gusted between them. "I'm not a virgin, but I feel so inept."

"You're not." He wanted to enclose her in his arms. Start with a kiss and get hotter and heavier from there. But he held himself back. This scene was hers to direct.

She stroked him. Up and down, her soft grip rolling over his thick head, tightening, then hugging back down his length. His breathing shortened until he was close to panting. Then she cupped his balls and gave them a squeeze.

His groan resonated through the night. Hopefully, Malcolm was asleep, but if he wasn't, that sound would let him know what was going on out here next to the ruined gardens.

When Sylva knelt, he blew out a hard breath and sucked a

new one in. Was she going to— Would she— She knew she didn't have to, right?

The anticipation of her mouth closing over his cock spread through him until he could hardly breathe. When she angled toward him and closed those pretty red lips around his tip, he squeezed his eyes shut. Seeing her go down on him would be the end.

He'd been sucked off, and it'd been just that. Getting off. Usually while the female got plowed from behind by his twin. He had Sylva all to himself. He had all of her attention. And her curiosity wasn't clinical.

Her arousal clung to his nose, sending more blood to his impossibly hard dick. As she took him deeper, she sucked harder. Forcing his eyes open, he looked down.

The expression of bliss on her face was his undoing. Her wet mouth sucking him, her hands kneading and massaging his sac uncoiled all the tension inside of him. Rocking his hips with her rhythm, he allowed himself to imagine all the forbidden things he wanted to do to her.

When had he started to think of her sexually? Not when they'd first met. She'd been a vulnerable prisoner. Not even when she'd first come into her power. He'd been so fucking proud of her.

It was later. When she'd seemed so far above him that he could climb forever and never reach her. When she'd looked at him as if he was the most unworthy male on the face of the earth, which had only confirmed what he already felt. Then again when he'd been watching over her and he'd *known* that yes, he was unworthy of her.

And she chose to be on her knees, taking him in, demonstrating just how much she really was the one in control of this situation.

"Sylva." He had to warn her, let her know that he was

going to come, and she had to decide whether to let it happen and how.

She opened her eyes and gazed up at him. On her knees, her mouth stretched wide, and her hands around him. Better than any fantasy he could conjure. He was done.

"Syl—" His climax slammed into him and he went rigid, his hips jerking.

She didn't let him go. Her strength surprised him once again. He tried to control himself but this orgasm shook him harder than any he'd ever had before. He wanted to twist his hands in her hair and thrust so hard that he choked her, but instead he managed to fist his hands at his sides and growl through the pleasure.

As his shudders faded, she released him with a pop, his cock bobbing in the night. But he looked at her again and was ready to go. She was fully clothed with blow-job-swollen lips and desire-filled eyes.

As he watched, her expression smoothed into the one she used in the Synod.

That was right. This was only for her, to let her use him for her needs. He'd been a fool to hope for more.

She rose in one fluid motion and tore her shirt off. "Lie down."

SYLVA PEELED her pants off before she could lose her nerve. The taste of him filled her mouth and his scent covered her. His erection hadn't faded. She could've sworn she'd done something wrong, but the power that had coursed through her as he came wasn't from her.

He'd felt pleasure—and a lot of it. Because of her.

Fuck you, Roman, and all your lies.

The night air felt cooler than it was. Heat poured through her and it needed an outlet.

Harrison stretched out across the lush grass. Her destroyed gardens were at her back and she'd take the metaphor and use it. Her past was behind her, and if the Raymore brothers thought they could come here and fuck with her life, then they could see for themselves just how well she'd moved on.

With a real male. A guy who didn't feel strong by making those around him cower. A shifter who was willing to put his ego aside and let her fumble through this.

And what a male he was. The extra shadows the night cast over him only added to his appeal. He was like her. Others assumed they knew him but they hadn't even scratched the surface.

She was naked and had all his attention. He propped himself on his arms with his legs stretched before him. And that erection. Hard, straining, and all hers to explore.

Something about him seemed unsettled, but he probably didn't let many females have free rein. He had a good sense of what others needed and he likely wielded that in bed, whereas she was driven by want and need and curiosity.

This level of autonomy in sex scared her as much as it fueled her. She got to do what felt good for her and she'd given him head. She'd chosen to—before they'd even started. Blow jobs used to be last on her list of preferred erotic experiences.

Being with Harrison cemented the realization that it wasn't the act that made someone feel good about themselves, it was the connection, the trust, and the mutual pleasure. She'd never grow a few inches until she was as willowy as she was curvy. But the way Harrison looked at her made her feel like the sexiest creature that had ever roamed the earth.

She knelt next to him once again and bent to land a kiss, stiffening when she remembered that she probably tasted like his release.

He brushed a finger down her cheek and looked deep into her eyes. "Do whatever you want with me, Sylva. I mean it."

"I taste like— I have your—"

"I know, and it's making me harder than I've ever been," he rasped.

She smashed her lips on his and the way he responded to her every lick and nibble relaxed her enough to stretch out over him. His erection pressed into her. Adjusting her legs until she straddled him, she rode his length.

It took only a few strokes to coat him in her wetness. Her body burned for more. Tactile stimulation wasn't the same as penetration and she wanted him inside of her, moving and stroking and filling.

She lifted her torso, pressing her fingers into his chest. "I'm ready."

He was holding his arms away like he was afraid he'd grab her and take over. "Do it." He twitched under her.

Rising, she grasped him and centered herself over his broad tip. This was it. She just had to press down.

But her body betrayed her. She couldn't move. She squeezed her eyes shut and opened them again. Harrison stayed still but concern was filling his gaze.

"I want to, but I can't." Tears threatened to fill her eyes. "I want to."

"Can I touch you?"

She paused, his question unexpected enough to jolt her brain out of the loop it was stuck in. "What?"

"I'll get you ready."

She wasn't ignorant, but what the hell did he mean? She was wet and naked and practically sitting on his cock. How could she not be ready? But between the two of them, he had more experience. "You can get me there?"

He slipped one hand between them and snaked the other around the back of her neck. Pulling her toward him, he waited until their lips touched and their tongues licked against each other before he slid a finger through her and circled her clit.

A ragged moan left her chest. Wasn't that just proof she was ready?

Maybe, but the more he rubbed, the more desperate she became. She'd had orgasms before and while they had felt good physically, they'd always been emotionally lacking. But the hot and sweet way he kissed her, combined with his sinful touch, connected all the missing dots.

She was swiveling her hips and grinding into him until she took him inside. The sensation of being filled only enhanced the wicked things his finger was doing.

Another groan and she sank down farther. Energy coiled inside of her with steamy promises of what was to come. Just a little shift down and a rock back and *ohhh…*

She had to break the kiss to rise up and ride him. Her hands were anchored on his chest as she worked his length and she kept her focus on them, concentrating on squeezing out every ounce of pleasure.

Pleasure turned to ecstasy the more he stroked in and out of her. He used just enough pressure on her clit to keep her from spiraling into her climax. It was all up to her.

She lifted her gaze to his. The concentration on his face, the way he held back to let her take the lead, and the awe— the awe got to her. In his eyes, she saw herself as the sensual shifter that she'd thought had been taken from her.

The explosion of ecstasy rocked her. She flung her head back and slammed into him as her inner walls squeezed and convulsed around him. Gasps and whimpers echoed into the night and she finished with a shout.

Sinking onto his chest, her orgasm subsided as she soaked in the heat of him.

As awareness came back to her, she noted one thing. He was still hard inside of her.

She lifted her head. "You didn't finish."

"I did earlier."

"But you need to again." Conflict warred across his face. "I know you wanted this to be my thing, but I don't want you to suffer."

"It's all right."

No, it wasn't. She didn't feel like a sexy shifter ready to take on the world of sex if she left her partner unsatisfied. "Harrison, I want you to come inside of me."

Resolve filled his eyes as he gripped her hips and took charge. She braced herself against him as he lifted and slammed her down.

So. Good.

She was slick and offered no resistance. He moved in and out, his thrusts growing stronger until his back bowed and he clenched his teeth.

Heat filled her as he came. She whispered his name and stroked his face.

Before tonight, she hadn't been interested in sex and hadn't been sure she ever would be. But tonight that doubt had been put to rest. She liked sex. She liked sex with Harrison.

CHAPTER 13

"Are you sure there isn't something you'd like to tell me?"

Harrison glared at Malcolm over the torn-up floor. It had been three days since the attack. Demke had arranged a delivery of luxury vinyl plank for Sylva's new floor. They didn't dare leave the place again, but delivery worked.

Demke had vetted the driver on his end. Malcolm had waited up the road and run alongside the delivery truck in the trees, using his senses to ensure it was the original driver and not one of the brothers.

Harrison glanced at the stairs. Sylva was downstairs, ripping up pickle-smelling carpet. "I don't have to tell you everything."

"Since when?" Malcolm sat back on his heels and wiped his brow. Harrison regretted waking up early to help with the remodel efforts before it was time for his shift. Malcolm was staying up late so they could overlap for a few hours and get shit done. "You told me when you met Gloria. You told me that you two had decided to wait until your mating night.

And you told me about her insecurity. After that," he shrugged, "there's been nothing to tell."

"Why bother when you obviously know?" He ripped up another plank, aiming his aggression at the flooring and not Malcolm.

Malcolm snorted. "Believe me, I can tell you two are fucking. It's hard to sleep through the medicine cabinet rattling as you rail her on the counter."

Harrison's cheeks burned, but not with embarrassment. The image of Sylva with her ass planted on the counter, her head tipped back, biting her lip to keep quiet, and her legs spread wide as he pounded into her, was enough to get him hot all over again. "Okay. So we're sleeping together."

"That's what I want to know." Malcolm leaned close, speaking low enough for only him to hear. "You're not sleeping together. It's business as usual until pants drop. Then it's back to pretending nothing's happening."

Leave it to Malcolm to cut to the heart of what was going on—and to know that it bothered him.

He should've said something, but it gave Malcolm the opening to keep going. "Let's not mention that she's the only one you've been with, you know, *by yourself*. Or that you're going back over and over again." He shook his head and yanked another board up. "Unless this counts as one *long* one-night stand, we both know that we don't re-tap the same well for very specific reasons."

Harrison tightened his grip on his plank of wood. "She wants to explore, all right?"

"I get that." Malcolm turned toward him, one knee on the subfloor and one arm draped over the bend of his other knee. "But does she realize what it's doing to you?"

"I'm fine."

"I won't bother to argue that you're not. Have you told

her you never slept with Gloria? Or that you haven't ever done more than casual and superficial?"

"Our sex isn't about me."

"The fuck it's not." Malcolm's voice was still a whisper, but barely. He clenched his jaw once before he kept going in a quieter tone. "She's not casual and superficial to you and she needs to know that."

Harrison crawled closer and gave his brother his most determined look. "She didn't have a choice before. She does now and she chose me—for a specific reason. I'm not guilting her into more."

"I think you're underestimating her feelings and yours."

"What feelings?" he hissed. "She doesn't have enough experience to know what she wants. When it comes to sex, she can learn that from me. When it comes to relationships, it'll have to be from someone else." His chest constricted as soon as he said it. A dull throb started in his fangs. If that imaginary male Sylva could practice romance with were outside, Harrison would need Malcolm to hold him back.

Malcolm studied him for too damn long. Harrison went back to ripping up the floor. Remodeling had come at the perfect time. It was an excellent way to funnel the restless energy that had filled him since that first time with Sylva.

He couldn't run. And the fact that he wanted nothing more than to lose himself in the woods for months while he figured out the mess in his head filled him with shame. He might've had a good reason to do just that before, when he was discovering romance and love, but it had been the worst thing he could've done.

Malcolm didn't push the subject. They got the rest of the entryway torn up. As they were hauling boxes of plank inside, a sound caught their attention at the same time. Both their heads swiveled toward the road.

Someone was coming. A pickup, but older than

Malcolm's. It ran rough, like it left a cloud of dark exhaust behind it. The speed it traveled was faster than Malcolm ever drove. There wasn't time to go inside and warn Sylva. Who and how many were unknown and Sylva didn't make rash decisions. She'd stay where it was safe. He'd wait out here with Malcolm.

The pickup rattled into the yard, an old beater that probably hadn't seen an oil change since the turn of the century.

Two shifters were inside, a male and a female. They didn't look much older than him, but their eyes said they were over a century old. Maybe two. They'd seen things and life hadn't been easy.

The guy killed the engine and got out. His bow-legged walk went with his overall grizzled look. He wore a plaid button-up top that was as old as the pickup and worn blue jeans. Piercing blue eyes gauged both him and his twin as he brushed the mop of dark hair off his face.

The female slipped out of the truck, much meeker than her companion. Her dark hair was pulled back in a ponytail and her hazel eyes were a swirl of brown and green. She was also dressed in a simple red plaid shirt and jeans, though cared for better than the male's.

The male glared at each of them. "Who the hell are you two?" Hostility rolled off him, whereas the female regarded each of them separately until her speculative gaze settled on him and she tilted her head.

"We're the ones who need to be asking that question," Malcolm said, a box of plank still in his arms. Harrison planned to use his as a weapon or toss it aside if this male caused trouble. "Who are you?"

Red flushed the male's face. "I don't need to answer. You both can take whatever you're doing here and leave."

Harrison didn't move and neither did Malcolm. Like they always did, Malcolm took charge and Harrison stood next to him as proof that whatever Malcolm ordered would get carried out without question. "You need to tell me who you are or get the fuck out of here and never come back."

The male blustered and stepped forward.

"Louis." The female's voice was full of censure. They were mates. He could smell the connection between them.

The warning glare Louis shot her made Harrison's hands curl into fists around his box. He pictured smashing it into the male's face. The guy didn't respect his mate and she clearly was the sensible one.

"Where's Sylva?" Louis demanded.

"Why are you asking?" Malcolm calmly countered.

"Look here." Louis stomped forward. He was at least four inches shorter than them, barely hitting six feet. Unusual for males of their kind, but not unheard of.

Harrison tensed, prepared to protect Malcolm as his brother set his box on the ground and changed his stance in case Louis tried anything.

Louis stopped five feet in front of them. "Go get Sylva and stay out of my business."

"Now how can I stay out of your business and get her at the same time?"

Harrison wanted to roll his eyes. This was Malcolm's favorite part, egging his adversaries on. Harrison would rather fight and get it over with.

"Louis, maybe we should've called first." The female's reasoning didn't go over well with her mate.

"Shut up, Marg."

Harrison growled and didn't bother holding it back.

Louis narrowed his eyes on him. "You got something to say, son?"

"I'm not your son," he snarled. Why'd he bother replying?

"If you were, you'd learn some respect."

Who the fuck was this male that thought he could get his way by force?

The front door to the house creaked open and Sylva's voice cut through the tension. "Father?"

⌇

HOW QUICKLY SHE'D REGRESSED. One look at Father glowering at Harrison and she'd been transported to her nineteen-year-old self, afraid to speak up, timid, and programmed to listen to those bigger and louder than her.

She was Sylva of the TriSpecies Synod. No more cowering.

She went down the three porch steps like she was the queen of England addressing a crowd. "What are you doing here?"

Father blinked at the hard edge to her voice. He should be shocked. During her time with Roman, he'd been her worst source of support. She'd cried and begged for him to find a way out for her and he'd chastised her.

Enough, child. If they hear you, we could all suffer. Be a good mate and he won't find fault with you.

And Mother. Sylva hadn't seen her since… That reason was better. No one knew her mother had helped her. At the time, she'd been so wrapped up in her own drama that she hadn't stopped to think about why Mother would bring up the idea of killing Roman.

Was Father just as bad?

Dismay stalled her footsteps. She'd been severely disappointed in Father for how he'd supported her mating, but to think that he could be as bad as one of them…

"Sylva." Mother's strangled cry cut through the tension and she propelled herself closer.

Harrison stepped into Mother's path and looked over his

shoulder at her. Mother pulled up short, fear making her eyes glisten. Father curled his hands into fists, ready to defend his mate.

"It's all right." Sylva's voice cracked.

Mother rushed around Harrison and threw her arms out. Sylva folded herself into the embrace.

"I missed you," she whispered. Growing up, they'd sought refuge in each other, daring to voice their opinions and criticize those in charge when no one else could hear.

Mother's shoulders shook and her tears scented the air. There was fear in them, and anxiety.

When they broke apart, she met Father's stern gaze. He looked so much older than she remembered. Gray peppered his hair and his shoulders were stooped like he carried the weight of the world.

"Father," she said coolly. Their relationship had changed when she'd learned her true mate was part of the leading clan of their colony. Giggles and games had been replaced with lectures about how a proper mate acted.

"Sylva." He no longer called her Bunny either, and he was the one who'd coined the nickname.

She didn't have to be a genius to read his expression and figure out why they'd come. "Did Grandma Raymore send you?"

"They just want justice." He didn't sound like he agreed with them. But he was here supporting them and not her.

"What happened was justice and what they're doing is illegal." She forced herself to stand her ground under Father's censuring stare and not run to Harrison's side. "When they're caught, they will be imprisoned."

Father's eyes widened. "You're a fool if you think—"

A growl cut through his words. Harrison planted himself between her and Father.

She was so tired of wanting more from her parents, only

to be left alone. "What am I a fool to think? Just in case I haven't learned to think for myself in the last few years, tell me."

Mother laid a hand on her arm. "He's worried, Bunny. We both are."

She looked from Mother to Father. Enough of this. They weren't here for her, they were here for *them*. Smoothly stepping away from Mother, she said. "Thank you for the warning. You may go now."

Mother's hand dropped to her side. "Sylva—"

Father took a step toward her. "You can't ignore this—"

She spoke over them both. "I'd invite you to stay, but my house is undergoing a remodel and we're short a room." They couldn't stay in her pissed-in room. She had her pride and she couldn't show her parents weakness. She turned to go back up the porch stairs. "There's probably a room at an inn in town."

Going into the house, she went straight for the bathroom. It was the first time she'd seen Mother since that night. And they were here to talk her into going back home. So she could what? Either be killed outright or mated off to someone else of Grandma Raymore's choosing?

If that happened, would Mother be there to pull the trigger again?

She'd stood up to them and it made her sick. She brushed at tears streaking down her face. The guys couldn't see her like this. They'd been working so hard with her and here she was crying over her parents' visit.

Her hands trembled as she ran the bath. Over the running water, the faint sound of an engine started and then faded into the night. They had left.

Heavy footsteps came through the entry, and then methodical sounds and murmuring. Someone went downstairs. Probably Malcolm going to bed for the night. Only Harrison would be out there.

She sank into the water, her skin turning red from the heat. A long soak while she gathered herself would help. It would be the first night since she and Harrison had started having sex that they wouldn't do anything. She desperately wanted to lose herself in his arms. But tonight, she needed to be alone with her thoughts, with her fears that she'd lost her parents to Four Claws' warped ideals.

Mother had risked everything to free her from Roman, and the first thing Sylva did upon seeing them, after years of being on the Synod and days of self-defense lessons, was to chicken out instead of returning to Four Claws where this had all started.

She should be proud she'd stood up to them, but instead, it felt like she was hiding behind her words like she was hiding in this bathroom.

CHAPTER 14

The night before had been quiet. Sylva had stayed in the bathroom for hours and then ghosted into the bedroom when he wasn't inside.

Harrison stared at the ceiling. His phone had buzzed with a message from Jonathon. No sign of Sylva's parents and none of them thought that was a good thing. Why come all the way down, only to talk to Sylva and shrug it off when she told them she wasn't backing down from the Raymores?

Why indeed.

Malcolm was on duty and tearing away at the floor. He was probably on the living room by now, and being on the noisy side was his way of telling his twin to get the hell out of bed. This thing with Louis and Marg was bothering him, too, otherwise Harrison would still be sleeping and the living room floor would still be waiting.

He blew out a breath and swung his legs down. His feet hit cold floor. Sylva had ripped out all the carpet in the basement already. To be fair, it had been old and sorely in need of an upgrade. The reason she'd had to change it out still raised his blood pressure.

Sylva.

How quickly he'd gone from detached when it came to females to torn up inside that Sylva hadn't come to him for anything. Not even sex. Her parents' arrival had bothered her and she'd shunned him.

He hadn't expected sex. He wasn't that inept when it came to relationships, but he was astute enough to know that if he and Sylva were in a relationship, she would've said something to him. Hell, she would've said good night. Or good morning. But she'd avoided him.

So much for even being friends.

Time to quit wondering what was going on with her and get to work. Prying hardwood up should work the angst out of him. He stepped into his jeans and grabbed a black T-shirt, giving it a sniff. Maybe another T-shirt. That one smelled like her.

He sifted through his clothing. They all smelled like her. He shrugged into one of Malcolm's navy-blue shirts and gathered up his clothing to wash.

After starting a load of laundry, he went upstairs.

"Sleeping Beauty awakens." On his knees, his back to Harrison, Malcolm was working up another plank in the middle of the living room.

"Were you afraid you'd get all this done and accidentally break a sweat?"

"Ha ha, jackass. There's a shitload of plank outside and I didn't want to haul it all in. It's ninety degrees out with almost as much humidity."

Or...he wanted to talk, and going downstairs to do it would signal to Sylva that they were talking about her. Hopefully the sounds of them tearing up ruined planks would be enough cover for their conversation instead.

He picked up the tool belt Malcolm had loaded for him and dropped to his knees beside his brother.

"I got Jonathon's message."

Malcolm whispered only loud enough for him to hear. "We should find out what's really going on with her parents. I notified Demke as soon as they left, and he's asked the local hotels to call if anyone fitting their description checks in. Synod business, right? "

"You don't think they reported back to the brothers and took off back to Four Claws?" Harrison said it as he yanked up a plank. They'd given Sylva's parents plenty of time to settle into the next phase of whatever the hell they were here for, but it didn't seem they'd settled anywhere.

"I don't think they're pro Raymore. I think they were told to come here and talk to their daughter or else."

"Then they can head home and never speak to her again." If they'd rather send their daughter to a family that wanted to harm her, then good riddance. They didn't have to be pro Raymore, but they were here, doing the family's bidding.

"Your attachment to her is clouding your senses." Malcolm slipped his gloves off and tossed them on the floor. He swiveled to face him. "They were terrified for her."

"They were afraid for themselves," Harrison hissed.

"That, too. But while Sylva was talking to them and you were being big bad bodyguard, I was studying them."

Harrison mimicked his twin's position. "And when you were studying them, did you notice how her father treats her mother? That's in front of people, in front of his own daughter. Did you look at them and think, these are two parents who raised their daughter just for a male they knew would use her?"

"Yes, idiot," Malcolm snapped, then dropped his voice again. "And there's a whole lot more there than meets the eye, but more than that, they're her parents. The Raymores can't get to her here. They don't dare face us. What does that leave two cowards to do?"

The reality of Malcolm's insight sunk in. *Shit.*

"Do you think they're safe?" Sylva's voice was shrill.

He and Malcolm spun around. She'd probably heard them arguing and snuck out of her bedroom, knowing damn well it was about her.

Malcolm sighed. "I think we should check on them, yeah."

Harrison rose. "I sent word to Demke that they were in town. He was going to see if he could find where they checked in to."

"He hasn't sent word yet." Malcolm straightened next to him and withdrew his phone from his pocket. "Nothing from Demke. You?"

Harrison shook his head.

"While I was sleeping, you all were looking for them?" Guilt and recrimination mingled in her gaze. She gathered herself, squaring her shoulders and adopting her default cool expression. "I'll call them." She disappeared and when she came back, her phone was to her ear. "No answer. They only have the one line."

Because that would be too much freedom for her mother. "Let's go." Harrison was already starting for the door.

"We can't leave this place unguarded," Malcolm said.

He gritted his teeth. One of them escorting Sylva wouldn't be enough. There were two brothers, and while Sylva could fight, it was too risky.

Sylva went for the door. "To hell with the house." She charged outside.

As they loaded up, Harrison had to note the level of concern Sylva had for her parents. She was wearing a paint-splattered T-shirt and jeans that had a hole in the knee. Her shoes were simple canvas slip-ons and her hair was hastily tied back in a low ponytail. If it weren't for her stunning eyes, any shifter in the area would look right past her and not register that it was Sylva from the Synod.

Malcolm flew down the gravel road to town and Harrison called Demke.

Demke's report was dismal. "I gave them some time before I reached out to each motel, but I've gotten no reports back that a couple matching their description checked in. I was going to try again, in case they had to check in with the brothers first or didn't want to pay for an extra night. It's a pretty poor colony they're from."

Which explained Sylva's expertise in gardening and preservation. When she was growing up, it had been a survival skill, not a fun hobby. Her mother probably had an even bigger garden and cellar.

The cab of the pickup was silent as they wove through town, looking for the old beater. The town was small and all shifter, but not a colony. Since it was where the Synod headquarters was stationed, it was full of families and businesses that served the Synod. There were three different motels in town, mostly to house those bringing official business in front of the Synod.

Once they'd cruised around the third motel, Malcolm headed back out of town. "We can either drive to their house, which is four hours of winding roads away, or go through the back roads around Sylva's place and search."

"We need to search. I can't go back home and wonder." Sylva cracked her window and searched their surroundings.

Harrison did the same. Malcolm drove slower.

When he turned off the highway, Sylva said, "There are only two other roads that shoot from this stretch." She was stating the obvious but she was probably worried out of her mind.

Malcolm took the first road they came to. Nothing but trees lined the road. No other traffic was around, and any other paths going off the road went to residences.

Backtracking, Malcolm took the second road. Prickles of

awareness covered his body. No new scents filtered in, but this had to be it. Unless Louis and Marg had driven through the night to get to Four Claws, they had to be around Tame Peaks, even if they were lingering just outside the city's limits.

"Look." Sylva pointed to a glint of metal up ahead. Malcolm let off the gas even though all of them wanted him to stomp on it and get there quicker. But it could be a trap.

As they rolled up onto the scene, the sour stench of the brothers became clear. The pickup was parked in the ditch, but it appeared parked deliberately, not crashed.

Two bodies were inside and slumped over. Malcolm hadn't parked yet, but Harrison hopped out. He didn't have to look to know Sylva did the same.

"Stay behind me." He held a hand out as if she couldn't just wind around him and run ahead. But she didn't. She swept along the road with him and down into the ditch as the smell of blood overwhelmed them.

They crept up to the vehicle. The brothers' body odors were there but fading. Her parents were inside the cab, unmoving. Malcolm's footsteps pounded the pavement as he rushed to catch up.

He went to the driver's side and pointed Sylva to go around to the passenger side. When he opened the door, he knew exactly what had happened. Louis was slumped over the wheel and Marg leaned against the door, her head falling forward. They'd each been shot, and since they were so still, the bullets must've been silver laced and a direct message to Sylva.

Sylva's tears spiked the air. She opened the passenger door and held her mother up. "Alive. Harrison, they're still alive."

∿

"SALT. I NEED SALT." She prodded at Mother's body, looking for any and all wounds.

Mother was cool under her touch, but Sylva sensed her heartbeat. Faint, but it was there.

Footsteps receded as Malcolm hurried back to their pickup. Harrison pulled Father out like he weighed nothing more than a fifty-pound sack of potatoes, then draped him over his shoulder. As Harrison carried her unconscious father out of the ditch and up to the box of the pickup, Malcolm dropped the tailgate so Harrison could lay Father down.

Malcolm's words carried on the wind to her. "Go get her mom. I've got this."

Relief flooded her. Salt was coming. Harrison appeared at her side, his hands clamping her biceps but not dragging her way. "Let me carry her. We can get them to the healers at the Synod."

Yes, the Synod. These were severe enough injuries to require extra help. And her parents would need to be in a place where the Raymore brothers couldn't get to them.

She nodded numbly and stepped out of the way. He lifted her mother under her shoulders and her knees and got her out of the vehicle without banging her head. Hours ago, she'd been filled with shame about how scared she'd been to even think about going back to Four Claws.

But her regret had been misdirected. The brothers weren't at Four Claws. They were somewhere near Tame Peaks. Using her fear, using her friends, using her family to get to her.

Rage kindled inside of her.

They rushed to Malcolm. Harrison stretched Mother out next to Father. Malcolm had dumped a nice pile of salt on Father's chest over the bullet wound. Turning, he didn't bother to move clothing out of the way before sprinkling salt over her mother's injured shoulder.

"I'll ride in the back with them." Sylva hopped over the edge and squatted down between their heads. Harrison moved their limp feet out of the way and closed the tailgate, then crawled in next to her.

Malcolm handed the round bottle of salt off and within seconds, they were back on the road.

The ride out felt ten times bumpier than it had on the way there.

She touched her father's cheek. Was it her hopeful imagination or was his color returning? She looked over her mother. No, she definitely looked better. "I think we got to them just in time."

"The brothers wanted to send a message," Harrison said. "If they'd wanted your parents dead, they would've used head shots."

The Raymores had been sending enough messages. And she was doing nothing but waiting for them.

Skills she would choose to use...

She had more to defend than just herself. She had to start thinking like the brothers, anticipating their moves. She had to remember that they didn't care about her and they didn't care about her parents. To them, the colony had always served their needs, and their needs alone.

This had to stop. Not just for her. For Mother and Father, who the Raymore family had tortured because of her. For the colony. For all the future mates like her that were to be herded off to their fates.

That family had had the upper hand for too long. She wanted to stop them more than she wanted to hide in a closet and cry. She was a shifter, a shifter with the ability to stop them.

Her parents' options were limited, but had they been

trying to send her a warning? Was she foolish to think her father had tried to take care of her in his own restricted way? She wouldn't know until he recovered, but memories flowed back.

Father never encouraged rebellion and especially discouraged speaking out against Roman or any of the others, but he had to have known that she and her mother talked. He had to have known how she and her mother were in agreement about the unfair power balance in the colony. Just like he had to know by now that her mother had helped her kill Roman. Yet, he was here with Mother under the pretense that he could talk some sense into her. He was doing exactly what the Raymores wanted him to, but was he up to anything else as well?

Mother was secretly subversive. Did Father play the distraction? Perhaps Mother had learned from him how to put on a show. He had more say and more power than she ever had, but not much. Did he use what he had to make it look like they were compliant little shifters while Mother moved in and taught her things like independent thinking?

She wanted a chance to find out. The salt had to be working.

The scenery flew by. Malcolm took the turn slowly to keep them from spilling out the back, but when they were on the straight stretches, wind whistled around them as their speed picked up.

She'd soaked in the bathtub for hours. Hiding. She'd been warm and safe and protected while her parents had suffered —because of her.

No more.

They approached the sprawling Synod building. Malcolm didn't take the loop to the main entrance like usual. He aimed for the back and his phone was up to his ear.

Every couple of seconds, Harrison's gaze swept over her

and her parents, but he concentrated on the area around them. While she'd been stuck in her own thoughts of how this could happen and all the nuances she had missed in her life, he'd been looking out for her, protecting them. If anyone was following, he would know.

She was so done with this. She was finished with needing constant protection and she was over being the victim.

Malcolm pulled to a stop by the back doors. The heavy metal panels swung open and a male and female shifter emerged. She recognized them, and if she tried, she could probably come up with their names. Two shifters had jumped to help her and her family. And she could hardly identify them. It shouldn't take nearly losing her loved ones to highlight a glaring deficiency in her style of leadership. She didn't need to keep everyone at a distance. Just because it was better than the style she'd grown up under didn't mean it was right.

Another pair of shifters wheeled two gurneys out. Had more come on duty for the emergency?

She vaulted out of the pickup box but hovered nearby as they loaded Mother onto one gurney and then Father onto the other. Harrison was at her back. Always the shield.

Before her parents could be wheeled inside, she grabbed one of the stretcher bearers by the bicep. "Please let me know how they're doing. Malcolm can pass my number along. Call me anytime, don't worry about the hour."

The male's stunned gaze jumped from her to Harrison. He dipped his head. "Yes, ma'am."

The four medics wheeled her parents inside and the door swung shut behind them. She shoved her hair off her forehead with both hands and turned to face the twins.

Malcolm's head was cocked, his brows drawn down. "Aren't you going inside with them?"

"No. Can you kindly pass along to Demke that I'd like my

contact information left with the team caring for my parents?"

"Absolutely."

"Sylva?" Harrison's tone was cautious, like he knew she was planning something.

"I'm done waiting. I'm done hiding. I'm not giving them another target." She stepped around to the pickup and whipped the door open. "Let's run home and grab our weapons. It's time to hunt."

CHAPTER 15

*H*arrison didn't like this one bit. But he had to acknowledge that it was a good plan.

Plan was perhaps too strong a word. They had gone back to Sylva's and grabbed all their weapons. He and Malcolm were both still in simple jeans and a T-shirt, but he now had knives strapped above each boot and two in his shoulder holster. His gun with silver-laced bullets was at his side.

Sylva had fewer weapons. Being a novice made it less likely that she would be the victor in a knife fight. Her best option was to shift and fight with the nature that drove her. Her lessons would come in handy.

And that was it. Their plan. They would drive back up to where they'd found Sylva's parents and follow the scent of Rafe and Clayton. Malcolm had reported to Demke. They had the support of the Synod. They wanted this over with, too—and if Sylva was involved in handling it herself, it'd look better to their people.

As always, Malcolm drove and he rode shotgun and Sylva was in the back. The windows were down, allowing the wind to tear through the cab. He caught a glimpse of her in the side-view mirror. Her hair was secured back in a ponytail, and she scanned the surrounding forest with a steely gaze.

No one had spoken unless it was to rattle off a list of supplies. They each carried a small pack of provisions like granola bars and bottles of water. And salt.

The only things they knew for sure about their opponents were that one of them had the ability to control animals and that they were working with silver. Since at least one of the brothers had been able to control Nala over such a long range, it could be safely assumed that the other brother's ability was amplification. But that was all they needed to know.

Malcolm propped his elbow on the door, his other hand loose on the wheel. "We hunt for them in our human form, do all the regulation Guardian bullshit, and from there it's like the Wild West. If they don't listen and follow our commands, then they need to be taken prisoner using whatever force necessary."

Harrison didn't think they would reach the prisoner stage. The resolve in Sylva's eyes and the feelings all three of them had about the brothers' tactics made the more likely outcome death, and he had no intention of allowing Sylva or his twin to die.

Stopping where they'd found her parents, Malcolm killed the engine. "This is as good a place as any."

All three of them got out. Sylva circled her parents' old truck, sniffing and inspecting it for any signs and smells that would aid them in their search. Harrison joined her as his twin made a larger arc around them.

"Rancid sweat, just like I remembered." She wrinkled her nose like it was the foulest smell in the world. And it wasn't pleasant. Her parents' fear clogged the cab and emanated from it several feet. Backing up, he was able to sift through the smells better.

Malcolm stopped and pointed north. A narrow deer trail wound through the trees, probably one the brothers had used to gain easy access to the road. "It's the strongest here."

She pushed off the pickup, adjusted her own backpack, and marched down the trail. Malcolm rushed in front of her and Harrison fell in step behind.

They had tracked several hundred yards when she said, "I feel better about this already."

"How so?" Malcolm asked.

Harrison knew what she meant without asking. Tracking down the Raymore brothers felt better than remodeling her house while wondering when they were going to have to rip out the floor again because it had been ruined once more.

"Taking action. I didn't do enough of it before, I don't do enough of it on the Synod, and I sure as hell wasn't doing enough for the last few weeks."

Malcolm glanced over his shoulder as he held some pine branches out of the way for her to duck under. "No one expected a single shifter to fight back against three brothers who were supported by an entire colony."

She didn't reply, but her boots ground harder into the dirt with each step.

"It's normal to feel like we should have done more," Harrison said quietly. "It'll never feel like enough."

Sylva looked at him from over her shoulder, her eyes appreciative. "Yes. Exactly."

This trek through the trees was eerily familiar. He was with his twin and worrying about the future of the female he cared about. Only this time he had a target. He had names. And he had scents.

He would not fail now.

And he had Sylva with him. She deserved to be part of this, she'd earned it, and it would do more to seize back control over her life than sitting in the Synod with armed protection. This was her fight and she refused to be left behind.

Gloria had refused to go with him. *Why can't your brother go and you stay?*

She's my sister, too.

But I'm your mate.

Always worried about herself. Gloria had gotten along with Camille, but she'd been so scared for herself.

She'd had reason to be, but she hadn't done anything about it.

Sylva had put herself at risk to protect others. She was with them to spare other shifters pain and suffering. There might've been parallels between Sylva and Gloria, but they were nothing alike.

SHE SHOULD BE CONCENTRATING on the search. And she was, but they were following a faint scent trail. There were miles to go and other than being on the lookout for predators under Rafe's or Clayton's control, there wasn't much to do beyond watching her footing.

At times, the trail was rugged and uneven, and then it stretched wide. Every so often, Malcolm would leave the path to ensure the brothers' scents weren't stronger elsewhere.

After a few hours of hiking, she gave up and let her mind mull over what it really wanted to.

Harrison.

He was usually quiet, but he was also distant. He'd been that way since they'd started sleeping together. Other than sex, he didn't offer more of himself, but it wasn't like they'd had the opportunity.

Last night would've been a good time, but she'd shut

herself off from him.

This search entailed finding the violent brothers of her equally abusive mate; she shouldn't be dwelling on what another male was thinking of her. But here she was.

Perhaps it was because her mate had claimed her early and she'd missed out on the running around, the multitude of affairs her kind enjoyed before settling down with that one special person. She was adrift now, wondering what it all meant.

Roman had been her one and only. She'd been born and programmed for him—though thanks to Mother, those teachings hadn't cemented like they'd been meant to. And thanks to Father, too.

The more she thought back on her upbringing, the more it all made sense. Long talks with Mother while Father stayed outside—their lawn had been immaculate in the summer. The looks exchanged with Mother when Father came into the room. At the time, Sylva had been panicking that he'd find out what she and Mother had said, the blasphemy they'd spoken about their leaders.

Each time, she'd worry Father would rain down one of his lectures, but after she'd learned to behave in public, he never had. It was like he and Mother had silently passed a baton. When he'd been done teaching her what the Raymores expected, Mother had taken over filling her head with resilience.

Thanks to those long secret talks, she'd rebelled, albeit passively, against Roman. After trying to legitimately be what he wanted and make him happy, she'd settled for claiming her independence in tiny ways.

Oops, I spilled this paint all over the orange carpet I never liked.

Roman, I heard someone at the store say John Todd should be the next leader, but I don't agree.

I just couldn't figure out how to unclog the vacuum. It didn't get done today.

She wasn't proud of not standing stronger, but if it hadn't been for her parents, she would still be married to Roman and doing her best to please his brothers—one at a time or all together. Whatever Roman wanted.

Guilt gnawed at her. If she hadn't kicked them out last night...

"It's not your fault." Harrison's deep rumble intruded on her thoughts. He had closed the distance between them without her noticing. Great hunter she was.

Malcolm was farther ahead. He'd hear them talking, but not the words if they kept their voices down.

"I should've seen what they did for me."

"If you had, they might've been exposed." Harrison's scent wrapped around her. They couldn't walk side by side, but he stayed close enough to talk. "Your mate would've known that you weren't brainwashed like he wanted."

"What would he have done, though? I mean, really? Treat me worse?"

"Yes. You and them. None of you would have survived."

She bit the inside of her cheek. It was easy to think she couldn't have had it worse, but yes. Roman would've leveled up in his abuse.

"Don't forget your role in the Synod is to keep this from happening again. To root out the dogma that drives isolated packs like the Raymores and the ones that killed Gloria. To stop them from taking over and strangling isolated colonies for generations."

That was her goal. Since this whole thing had started, she'd been falling short of that goal. But one thing was clear —if she survived, she was going to go after those isolated colonies. She'd visit each one of them and listen to the voices that didn't get a chance to be heard.

The path took a steep uptick and they had to spread out and watch their footing. When they reached the top, Malcolm let out a low whistle.

"Their scent is stronger up here, but not strong enough for them to be around." Malcolm disappeared around some trees. "And there's a cabin. An old one."

She rushed after him, Harrison close behind.

Her first impression of the cabin was that it was indeed very old. She wasn't acquainted with the history around here. This place could've been built by loggers or rogue shifters who'd wanted to live off the grid and not claim a pack. The walls were composed of rustic lumber and the window was a single sheet of cloudy glass.

Raymore stench surrounded the place, but like Malcolm said, it wasn't strong enough to indicate either brother was around. Had they controlled Nala from this far away? They had to be twenty miles as the crow flies from her house.

No. If they weren't here, then there was another location they lurked in, one that was probably closer to her house.

She stopped in the clearing around the little structure. Trees had grown back in the once felled area, crowding the cabin. They were thinner but scaled to the sky.

"This would be a quaint place if weren't for the Raymore taint," she said.

"Agreed." Malcolm dropped his pack. "I'll take a look inside."

Harrison dumped his pack in the same spot and she followed suit. She wasn't going to let them do all the work. Taking the inner perimeter, she searched for signs of what the brothers were doing here other than sitting on their asses and thinking of ways to torture her.

Harrison drifted in and out of the trees. She would've missed him if she weren't so attuned to him. His dark shirt and dirt-smudged jeans blended well and he didn't make a sound.

Malcolm appeared in the doorway. He was swinging the door back and forth. "Huh. They oiled the hinges to keep from making a sound."

Harrison emerged from the darkness of the forest, squinting at the sky. The sun was setting. It'd be dark soon and they'd have nothing but the stars to guide them. "They probably wanted to be prepared in case we found them."

"Well, they lived like pigs." Malcolm swung the door wide open, giving the cabin as much air as possible. "No campfire, wrappers are all over in here, and they must've used their mind control to keep bears from pillaging the place. Empty tuna cans have been dumped in the corner."

She folded her arms across her chest. Memories assaulted her. Beer cans getting tossed on the floor. *Get that, will ya, Syl?* Most of the time, they hadn't bothered to ask. "I would say that they might've been masking their scent, but they're really slobs."

Finding the cabin meant they were close, closer than they'd ever been to finding them. But it was empty. Did the brothers happen to be out, or was her determination to hunt them down all for nothing? Was she still the one being hunted?

CHAPTER 16

*H*arrison roamed through the trees. It was after midnight and Malcolm and Sylva were camped in the cabin for the night. He and Malcolm were splitting four-hour shifts so each of them could get rest.

None of them was going to relax enough for sleep.

From here, the only direction they had to go was deeper into the forest. Farther away from civilization. Being this isolated made him twitchy. If Sylva had stayed back, he'd probably be vibrating out of his skin.

He and Malcolm had grown up like this. This should feel like coming home, whether he was hunting anyone or not. But he'd come to prefer the proximity of his fellow Guardians while at the same time relishing time away, like traveling to Synod headquarters and around the area on assignments. He was constantly around people, not blocked off from information, and most of all, and he got to see his parents once in a while.

He liked his life. Huh. He'd never thought about it like that, but once he'd let Sylva in, he could see everything he had instead of all he'd lost. But with the way she'd avoided him last night, had he even had her in the first place? Was he just a placeholder?

He scrubbed his hands over his face. This was what being in the dark all alone did to him.

The cabin door whispered open. Malcolm would have been stealthier.

Harrison made his way back toward the cabin. Sylva met him halfway.

"I can't sleep." Her weapons were still in place. Good. There was no pajamas or getting comfortable on this excursion.

"Malcolm?"

"Dozing. I told him I was coming out for air." She strolled around the cabin. "I can't believe they didn't have a campfire or anything."

"They were probably in wolf form most of the time." Judging by all the trees that had been sprayed with urine, they'd also marked everything they could. "Someone might've noticed the smoke and come looking."

She tilted her head back. "I doubt they admired the view at all. Can you believe the Milky Way this time of year?"

He never stopped to look at the stars. When he'd been searching for Camille, he'd used them for light, navigation, and the target of his curses. "They're nice."

Her smile was serene. "Yes. They are. Looking at them reminds me that in the grand scheme of things, this is just a blip." She sucked her lower lip in and worried it with the point of a canine. He had to look away. He wanted to do the same thing. "Thank you. For helping me, you know..."

"Anytime." Was this her *You're nice and all, but I won't be needing your services anymore* speech?

"No, I mean it. I don't think I would be out here without your support, in that way. But overall, your help and

Malcolm's advice—I can't believe how wrong I was about you two."

He withdrew the emotional part of himself from this conversation. How could he complain? Someone like Sylva wasn't scared of him and she didn't hate him. She seemed to like him. Had he expected her to fall madly in love with him? Hadn't that been the last thing he wanted from any partner?

Or had he been afraid that he'd be the one falling hard and the female would slap him on the ass and say, "Good game"? Because that's what was happening.

"Don't worry about it." That came out way too rough. Would she take it in an *aw shucks* kind of way?

She stepped closer. "So many people are wrong about you."

Panic infused his blood. He didn't need to hear how misunderstood he was. He didn't care. She didn't need to tell him he was nice and to leave and meet someone new. He backed away. "No, they're not wrong."

She blinked and frowned. "Harrison, I thought—"

"You're strong. I wouldn't be doing my job if I let you think otherwise." That had come out wrong. Sleeping with her hadn't been part of his job. But as a Guardian with the Synod, he and Malcolm had been teaching self-defense classes and building shifters up. They were strong creatures and their own leaders had made them feel otherwise for too long. "Sylva—"

"No." She let out a bitter chuckle. "I'm not versed in the ways of our kind when it comes to sex. It appears I put too much thought into what we were doing."

He shook his head. Did she think there was more between them? She hadn't acted like it. Did she truly want more?

His hopes lifted but he squashed them down. She didn't

want to hurt his feelings and was letting him down easy. Of course she wasn't interested in more with him than sex.

"Sex for me isn't about feeling." It was about forgetting that he wanted to feel. How could he explain it? Did he want to? "It isn't about relationships. It's not even about friendships."

Hurt rippled through her features. "I guess I'm not that kind of shifter."

"And you shouldn't be." She was more than an orgasm. When she came, it was like the sun shone on his soul. When she smiled and those shadows left her eyes? He lived for those moments. But he was not going to let her think that she should stick it out with him because she felt guilty for misunderstanding him.

The cabin door swung open and Malcolm stormed out, stabbing a hand through his hair. "Sweet Mother Earth, Harrison. Do you insist on being both dense and stubborn?"

He scowled at his twin. "Stay out of it."

Sylva backed away like she was trapped between two predators. And she was, but it was the safest place for her.

Malcolm flung an arm out at Sylva. "Tell her."

He ground his teeth together. His canines were going to puncture the inside of his lips if he didn't let off the pressure.

Sylva's gaze swiveled between the two of them. "Tell me what?"

"Malcolm..."

His brother ignored the warning in his voice. "How many females have you had sex with that weren't in a threesome— or more—with me? Just you and someone else?"

It wasn't dark enough to hide Sylva's adorable blush.

Malcolm cupped a hand around his ear. "What was that? Just Sylva? That must mean she means something to you. And how many times did you sleep with Gloria?"

"I'm going to kill you." But he was rooted in place, horrified, embarrassed, and enraged that Malcolm would dare butt in like this.

"What? Gloria wanted to wait? And you felt that if she couldn't have the experience, you shouldn't either?" Malcolm drew back like he'd detonated a bomb and wanted to watch the fallout.

Sylva's brows drew together. "Is that true?"

Humiliation closed in until it was a struggle to draw breath. "We were young. She thought our day should be special. But then… I left."

"I'm not leaving until you tell Sylva you like her." Malcolm shoved his hands into his pockets.

"We're not in grade school." Harrison's cheeks were burning. He'd grown a beard because he didn't care about his appearance, but hiding his blush was an even better reason for it.

Sylva's gaze was on him, but he was too much of a pussy to look at her.

"Perhaps I should go inside," she said and turned away from him.

"Don't." She stopped. He couldn't let her leave thinking that he really didn't care about her. If she rejected him, he'd deal with it like an adult. "Don't go."

He opened his mouth to say, "I like you," when what he really meant was that his world revolved around her. He counted down the minutes until he could be with her and only felt complete when he was buried inside her strong body. He wanted her to trust him. With her safety, with her life, with her heart.

But a familiar, foreboding smell wafted across his nose. He reached for the gun in his holster and spun toward the trees. "Get in the cabin, Sylva."

~

SYLVA RAN FOR THE CABIN, her heart in her throat. They were coming. Rafe and Clayton were close enough to smell.

A roar made her jerk around and stumble backward. She almost fell on her ass, tripping over the threshold.

That sound hadn't come from a shifter.

"Bear," Harrison said to Malcolm.

The twins sauntered around the clearing. Only because she'd come to know them so well could she tell how tense they were. Their eyes reflected in the moonlight, their hands steady as they kept their weapons aimed toward the ground, their steps light.

She exited the cabin. "I didn't hike all this way to hide."

Pulling her top off, she flung it inside. She tossed her two knives on top. Her pants and boots followed. She shifted and went to stand between the twins. They each looked at her but didn't shoo her away.

Her senses were more acute in her wolf form. Branches cracked as the bear charged through the trees, its breath huffing like a wild beast.

"You distract the bear," Malcolm said to her. "And don't forget they have a gun with silver-laced bullets. Stay low and keep moving."

She dipped her head and trotted in random patterns.

The pungent scent of bear grew stronger. All she had to do was be faster and more agile...in the same forest the bear lived in and knew intimately. Great.

She gave herself a shake. As long as she stayed clear of silver, the bear could maul her, but given enough time to heal, she'd be fine. The Raymore brothers could command it to do just that, but they'd be busy with the twins.

While her running might be erratic, she was sniffing the air with purpose, determining where the brothers' smell was stronger. She hit on their scent and concentrated. The bear was coming right for them, but the stench of smelly shifter was stronger on the other side of the cabin.

Snapping limbs echoed through the night. The huffing of the bear was audible before it charged into the clearing. Its sides heaved and its dark eyes were wide, crazed. The poor thing might die of a heart attack before it got a claw in her.

She yipped and zigzagged in front of it before darting to the side. One mighty paw swiped out, missing her haunches. She'd done enough to catch its attention. Sprinting for the trees, she didn't have to look back to know it was following her. The ground shook under her feet.

Damn, bears were fast.

Bunching and stretching, running at full speed through the forest in the middle of the night was the craziest thing she'd ever done. It wouldn't do any good to outrun the mind control. They'd held on to Nala for miles. And she didn't want to get lost in the forest and not know what the outcome of the fight was. She made figure eights around trees, wove through branches, any path that would force the bear to slow down and calculate its footing.

A shot rang out. She almost skidded to a stop. The bear was as startled as she was, but the noise wasn't enough to shake the mind control.

And they were back to the cat and mouse game.

Fatigue dogged her. She had plenty of stamina, but going at full effort was taxing and the terrain was uneven, requiring all her abilities and total concentration. The bear was starting to weave and stagger. If she survived this, she'd kill a deer for it. As it was, all the deer had probably been smart enough to run far away after smelling the Raymore brothers.

Another gunshot and she couldn't help herself. She veered toward the cabin. In her haste, she stumbled over an exposed root and went tumbling. The bear loomed over her, froth coating its mouth. Claws that could rip out her throat flared out and were crashing down. She rolled, but her back was scored. She yelped and twisted, but there wasn't an immediate follow-up attack. The bear was shaking its head and snuffling.

It met her gaze and its eyes were clear, but exhausted. She carefully rolled to her feet, ignoring the searing pain in her hide. Calling on her own ability, she lowered her gaze and skirted a few feet away. Submission. She wasn't a danger.

Another gusty exhale. She looked toward the cabin and whined. Danger.

The big, shaggy head swung in the same direction. She circled farther away and sat to show him she respected his size and dominance.

Somehow, her communication got through his terror. He lumbered away from the cabin, limping and zigzagging.

She staggered to all fours. The cuts were deep, but not fatal. She'd heal.

Sticking close to the trees, she made her way toward the cabin while staying concealed. She'd find out what was going on, who was doing the shooting, before she charged in to help.

She inhaled. So much blood. Four different shifters plus her. None of them was getting out of this unscathed.

The stench of death greeted her. Her heart rate kicked up. Was it just the brother that had controlled the bear? She lifted her snout and sniffed. Too many injuries to tell.

She crept forward until she had a decent view of the fight. Two prone figures were on the ground, but only one of them was moving. Malcolm, crawling toward the cabin.

Harrison was tangled in a fight with… She squinted. Rafe. The guy had always been a brute and he fought dirty. Each male wielded a knife and their fangs.

She glanced at Clayton. He must've been the one to

control animals. He was nude with a neat gunshot in one side of his head and a not so neat hole out the other side. Had he been in shifter form when he'd charged?

She stepped out. Malcolm needed help. Rafe barely spared her a glance, but his eyes were packed with hate and fury. Yet he could do nothing to her while fighting Harrison. She trotted to Malcolm and nosed him in the shoulder to let him know she was there. The smells were too chaotic to determine proximity.

"Silver," he gasped. His shoulder was ripped apart and he had a stab wound in his thigh. He'd sacrificed himself to shoot the wolf going after Harrison and taken a stab wound for the team.

Darting into the cabin, she found the container of salt. She shifted into her human form and opened the spout. Running back out to Malcolm, she dumped the salt on his shoulder.

He groaned and tried to roll away. "Fuuuuuck."

That was a good sign, right? She scanned the yard. The glint of metal caught her eye. One of the guns.

Thuds and grunts filled the night. She scurried to the weapon, oblivious to her nudity. This was a good way to cure her self-consciousness.

Her hand was shaking when she reached for it. The years peeled away until she recalled the sight of her hand gripping another handgun. Except Roman's had been a silver pistol. This was sleek and black. Modern.

Self-defense was about learning the skills she would choose to use in a fight. But she would never have chosen to use a firearm—a skill she didn't possess in the first place. And this wasn't self-defense. This wasn't a situation she could command her way out of.

This was survival—hers and the twins'.

She had no clue about safeties or ammo or how to tell if a

gun was loaded and ready to fire. She'd just have to learn on the fly, and remember what Mother had taught her about guns years ago—lessons she'd never been brave enough to use.

Steadying her hand with her other, she waited for a break in the fight, waited for her moment. Her gut twisted and she saw Roman's face in front of her, laughing about how weak she was, how she could never pull the trigger. How he'd spare her if she put the gun down.

Only your bitch of a mother will pay.

The gunshot from years ago rang in her ears until she couldn't decipher what was happening in front of her now and what had happened then.

She blinked and squinted. Roman is dead. *You can't even aim properly. Look how you're holding that thing. Can you live with killing me, Bunny? Can you kill your unarmed mate?*

She shook her head, her vision clearing in time to see Rafe slice down, the metal of his knife glinting in the starlight. Harrison danced back and kicked out. His boot hit Rafe in the gut. Stumbling back, Rafe snarled. He plowed to a stop and crouched to charge Harrison.

This was her moment. She lifted the gun. But the truth of Roman's words echoed in her head. Killing him had taken everything away from her. For years, she'd seen him drop every time she shut her eyes.

Rafe sneered in her direction, readjusted the knife, and stalked toward her.

"Unload the clip in him," Harrison barked at her.

Rafe was drawing near. "Sure you can do it yourself?" Bloody spittle covered his mouth as he laughed. "Why don't you give the gun to one of your bodyguards?"

Harrison's lips thinned and he attacked. Rafe spun and plunged into Harrison's gut.

"No!" She'd screwed up her chance. She'd failed just like Roman had said she would.

Malcolm was next to her, swaying on his feet. He lifted the gun from her numb fingers and aimed. How could he shoot? The males were tangled together.

Harrison dropped to a crouch and the gun fired three times. Rafe jerked with each shot.

Harrison shoved him off and rolled backward out of the way, but he didn't pop up.

She could do nothing but stare as Malcolm retrieved the salt for Harrison. Both Raymore brothers had silver-laced bullets in their heads and both had managed to die looking just as violent in death as they had been alive.

Taking a life shouldn't be easy. But she hadn't managed to do it to save herself, or even the male she was falling in love with. Roman was still in her head when it counted the most.

She didn't know how long she stood there. Then Harrison was next to her, his hands on her shoulders. "It's over," he murmured. "It's over."

CHAPTER 17

This was the most the Synod had ever heard him speak. Harrison sat on a chair, facing the panel of five. Malcolm was next to him as they recounted the fight.

It hadn't been forty-eight hours since Rafe and Clayton were terminated. He, Malcolm, and Sylva had finished their rations to spur healing and started the hike back to Malcolm's pickup. Once they'd found a nice place to camp, they'd passed out until morning, then finished the long hike.

Malcolm had given up on conversation after the first few miles. Sylva had been stuck in her head and Harrison had a good guess why.

Instead of going to Sylva's, they'd gone straight for the Synod. They'd cleaned up, patched their clothing where needed, cleaned their weapons, and slept. So much sleep.

As soon as they'd arrived at headquarters, Sylva had gone to check on her parents, and again when she'd woken. They were almost completely recovered and she'd spent the rest of the day with them.

He couldn't forget the conversation they'd been in the middle of when they'd gotten jumped.

Up on the dais, Sylva was quiet, her eyes downcast as he recounted the fight. Demetrius and Jonathon looked like they could be passing a bowl of popcorn. They'd stopped him with twenty questions already about technique and style and more details than Harrison thought were important. He wrapped up the story and pressed his lips shut.

With the exception of Sylva, they seemed satisfied with the outcome. It made no difference to them whether Sylva had pulled the trigger or not, but Harrison had glossed over that part.

Demetrius tapped his hands on the tabletop. "I vote for you two to be the ones to go to the colony and inform them of the change in leadership, effective immediately. They'll need to decide on a new leading clan, with a leader who is not a Raymore."

Jonathon inclined his head. "I agree. It'll make more of a statement, as well as stress our message that they must allow and facilitate access to the Synod's resources for their residents."

Harrison wanted nothing more than to march into Four Claws and tell them how it was going to go. But there was that talk with Sylva.

Demke glanced at Sylva. "Unless you feel like you require their services?"

Sylva worried her lower lip, but she shook her head and summoned a small smile. "It will be quiet, but I will be fine. And I'll tell John Todd about his brothers. Later."

He didn't blame her for waiting. John Todd would sniff out the fact that she hadn't killed either brother and taunt her with it. She needed to fortify herself against him first.

"When would you like us to go?" Malcolm asked.

"As soon as possible." When no one else added their thoughts, Jonathon continued. "Don't give them time to reorganize. I'd rather they learned from us that Rafe and Clayton are dead."

This was not a new assignment for him and Malcolm. They often went to small colonies on behalf of the Synod to open up communication, sometimes with discussion, other times with a heavier hand. But this time, it was personal. As if he hadn't understood before how important it was that packs had to answer to an authority beyond their borders. This time, he'd seen firsthand why it was critical.

Demke rose, signaling their dismissal. "Clear your things out of Sylva's and notify me when you head out."

Harrison and Malcolm walked out with Sylva. The sun had already set, but it was only eleven at night. The late meeting had been for the vampires, but it had also allowed them to rest up.

Malcolm tossed him the keys. "I'll have Demke take me back to the apartment. Pick me up on the way out of town. You two can talk and shit."

Harrison stiffened. Talk. Picking up where they'd left off. It was time to be honest with himself. And her.

"Malcolm," Sylva began, "never let it be said that I don't appreciate your subtlety."

He spread his arms. "I've heard it's my best quality."

Harrison glared at him, nerves rocking his body like the time he'd taken the blame for ruining Maw's rose bushes.

Sylva climbed into the pickup. He got behind the wheel, fired up the engine, and pulled away. She propped her arm on the side of the door. Her dark hair blended in with the night and her eyes reflected the streetlights as he flew through town. Now or never.

"Sylva—"

"Was I special?" They were on the highway now, and without the streetlights, her expression was concealed in shadow.

"Yes." Then he said deliberately, "You *are* special."

She looked at him. "You really haven't been with anyone on your own?"

For once, he let himself talk about her, about them. "Gloria and I were teenagers when we met. My family rarely ventured into town, but Malcolm and I were young males getting restless. I saw her crossing the street and I knew. She wasn't like the other females, and at first it was just what I wanted. Then…"

"She was a victim of her birth?"

He chuffed out a breath. "Yeah. If she'd been born to any other family, she could've lived in peace. But she was determined to make her parents proud. She was just as determined to prove herself."

"So she kept herself distanced from you to prove she could stand on her own, while relying on you to scare away anyone who'd hurt her."

"Yep."

"I'm like her."

He was going to deny it, but he wasn't sure what answer she wanted from him. "In some ways." She didn't reply and he sifted through his head for something to say. All he could come up with was "How are your parents?"

"Good." Her voice lightened but was it just artifice? "Really good. They're so relieved. And so proud." *They shouldn't be* went unsaid but he'd bet she was thinking it.

They fell quiet again. Was this how Malcolm felt when there was silence, jittery and uncomfortable? He said the first words that came to mind. Important words. "I like you. And not because you're like Gloria. I like you because you care about others. You're kind and sexy and you make me feel… like myself."

She was staring at him. He wanted to face her, but he'd go off the road. Or stop the pickup and take her right there on the side of the road—if she'd let him. He needed to show her how he felt.

"It wasn't just empowering sex for me. I wanted to be with you." Her tone wasn't shy. It was strong. Firm. Decisive. "I still do. The way you make me feel…" She sighed. "Like myself. Like it's okay to *be* myself. I'm just really tired of pretending and I don't have to do that with you."

"I count our walks at night as the favorite time of my life." More had to be in his future. Had to.

"Can you… Can we… before you go, can we be together?"

His body lit up like a holiday parade. He wanted to be with her, too. And while the time by the ruined garden was special and their stolen moments against the bathroom counter and out in the garage had been amazing, he wanted to…he wanted…

To make love, dammit. Nice and slow.

He pulled into her yard and parked in the usual spot. Killing the engine, he let the quiet of the night seep into the cab. "Malcolm won't mind if I take a little extra time."

He slipped out and got to her side before she could open the door. Helping her out, he did his best impression of a gentleman, which was mimicking Malcolm in this case.

Sylva smiled at him, but his good manners only went so far.

"I wanted slow and easy," he growled, picking her up, "but I think just getting you to a bed will have to be enough for now."

She wound her arms around his neck and hooked her legs around his waist. "We'll have more time when you get back." She planted her mouth on his.

A slither of unease passed through him like ghosts from his past. He was leaving her. But she was safe. She wasn't begging him to stay.

It was his senses that got him up the porch stairs to

unlock her front door. Pushing through the entry, he kicked his boots off and went straight for the spare room she'd been using. Spreading her out on the bed, he stood back and rolled his tattered T-shirt up. She propped herself on her elbows, her silky hair falling back. Her curvy body was on display—but she was still clothed.

Less than a day ago, a bear had been chasing her and he couldn't get to her. But she'd survived and she'd run back to the fight. He had to see her now. Ripping his shirt off, he growled, "Take your clothes off."

She stretched up to lift her top over her head. He couldn't pull his gaze away as she kicked her boots off and shimmied out of her bottoms. Somehow, he'd managed to strip himself. He crawled onto the bed and over her.

He'd never had such an urge to plunge inside a female and let his body take over, to release only so he could start over. But he held himself off her and saw to her pleasure first.

Starting with a kiss. Long and sensual until she was clinging to him. She slid her legs up and down his, but he couldn't lower himself or he'd be a goner.

"Spread your legs for me, Sylva."

She did as he asked without hesitation. Leisurely, he made his way down her body. Their previous times together had been about what he could do for her, but this was about how good it could be between them. How good they could be for each other. How they could communicate when words failed.

I like you didn't come close to his feelings for her. He knew her scent, her expressions, when she needed a little more support and when she could conquer on her own. He knew her body, her taste, and how she arched just before she came. He knew that she wanted to be held afterward but was too afraid to ask. His own insecurities at the time had made him wonder if she'd just wanted to get away without hurting his feelings.

But there'd be holding tonight. He and Malcolm might not be able to leave until dawn.

Pressing a kiss over her navel, he wedged himself between her thighs and gazed up at her.

Her skin was flushed and desire filled her violet eyes.

"I'm going to make this good for you," he said. There was no reason not to, and talking during sex had never been his thing, but he was different with her.

"You don't have to try too hard."

"Like this?" He dipped his head and licked through her until he landed on her clit.

She bucked against him. "Oh, god. Just like that."

She was wet and responsive and no, he wouldn't have to do much before she was coming on his tongue. Forcing himself to slow down, he strung out her pleasure. He refused to think his past was useless. If it had taught him the skills to show Sylva how much he cared about her, then so be it. He called on every single trick he'd ever learned.

"Harris—Harrison!" Sylva squirmed, but he held her tight. Her hands were twisted in his hair and she rode his face, searching for her release.

Not yet, honey.

He slid a finger inside her and groaned. Wet, hot, and tighter than he'd ever felt. She was coiled and ready to blow.

He set a steady pace and backed off with his tongue.

She rocked her hips once, then again, and a long groan left her as she arched her back.

There it was. His beautiful shifter was climaxing. Letting his finger do the rest of the work, he looked up and watched as her eyes fell closed and she moaned his name over and over. Her body shook and when she was done, her legs went lax.

"That was amazing," he said as he slipped his finger out and heaved himself over her.

Her scent coated his face, his beard, but neither one of them ever cared. Trailing her fingers over his beard, she murmured, "It was amazing for me. You did all the work."

He touched her forehead with his. "And for me. Giving you pleasure means a lot to me. I get to watch you come. I treasure it." Look at that. Give him Sylva and an erection and he couldn't shut up.

"Harrison," she breathed. "Oh, my Harrison." She wrapped a hand around his cock and guided him inside. "I treasure you, too."

She cupped his face as he pushed in and out of her. His body trembled, taking it slow, but of all the times he'd had sex, this was not the time to fly apart and climax in a few thrusts.

She met him for every thrust, kissing his chin, the corners of his mouth. Wrapping her legs around his waist, she dug her heels into his ass.

So beautiful. Her hair spread around her like a black velvet cloud. He dropped his head and scraped his chin along her collar line as he nibbled her satiny skin, knowing damn well it drove her crazy.

She shuddered in his arms. "That's just naughty." But it had the desired effect. She tensed tighter around him, inside and out.

He turned over the reins to her body. His hips jacked in and out and she coiled harder around him. Their peaks were imminent and with his face at the crook of her neck, a new sensation took over.

He wanted to mark her. His jaw flexed. Marking a female was like both a promise ring and a tattoo with his name on it. They'd only just confessed that they liked each other, though he hadn't come close to saying how he really felt.

In this bed, he said it all. His body was all hers. But his mind… He had to open himself to her first, give himself to her, trust himself with another female again.

"Do it." She cupped the back of his head without missing a beat. "Claim me."

Mine. He clenched the bedding between his fist but continued to hammer into her. Do it. All he had to do was bite down.

"We both know this is special. Mark me." She said it in her commanding voice.

This was the female for him. But as he opened his mouth again, all he could think about was another female who'd relied so completely on him.

SYLVA WANDERED around the garden with Mother. Father roamed the yard, looking at the property. She touched a spot on her neck, the one Harrison had left unmarked, for the twentieth time since he'd left.

He'd tried to explain. She'd said she understood, but when he'd driven off, she'd felt less special. They both had baggage and it was possible that their luggage wasn't going to match.

Mother pointed at the remnants of the strawberries. "At least you know those will come back. The raspberries, too. And rhubarb. Not even shifters can kill rhubarb."

Sylva stopped to glower at the decaying plants. Once a bumper harvest, it had turned to compost. "The fruit I'm not worried about. I'm almost over mourning the loss of the veggies. You should've seen the tomatoes."

"Do you sell your stuff?"

"I preserve what I'll eat for the next few years and then bring the rest to work." Where they had a pantry for shifters who came to them hungry. No one told them who donated the food. It was better that way.

"You'll be starting over."

Yep. Her pantry was now empty, clean, and smelling like pickles.

"I can help with that," Mother said quietly. "If you'd like."

Father sauntered over. "I will, too." She stared at him, but he wasn't looking at her. "Tell us when you want to plant and we'll come back."

Father digging in the dirt? Gardening was considered too menial for the head of the family. The task had been relegated to her and Mother. A duty they hadn't had a choice in, but had loved. Gardening was their reprieve. It was outside, too public to talk, but she and Mother worked in harmony.

It the kitchen, where they processed the food—that was a different story.

"I'd like that." She smiled at Father. "You two are welcome here. Anytime."

Mother turned from the plot. "Actually, we've been discussing changing packs and moving here. Now that it's possible with the Synod's interference."

"There are a few rentals in town," Father added. "And I managed to keep some money out of the Raymores' greasy paws."

"It wasn't easy." Mother and Father exchanged a knowing look. "Shawna is ferocious when it comes to payments. She can smell a lie better than the rest of her pack."

Father nodded. "Which made her a good tax collector."

Exactly why Sylva championed the needs of those in isolated packs. "No one should be going door-to-door, bullying the population in the name of tax collection." She shook her head. "I almost wish I had gone with Harrison and Malcolm, just to see her face when he tells her that her family's reign is over."

All those times Shawna had snidely commented about real power having to be earned. That the Raymores could earn it, but people like Sylva and her parents were born to be pawns.

Born to be pawns.

"Why are so many of our mates born within the colony?" Living among her own kind in Tame Peaks and working for the Synod, she'd spent years listening to their stories and learning how their world was really supposed to work. She hadn't thought about that unique aspect of Four Claws before because that had been her normal.

Then Harrison had shared how special he'd felt, finding Gloria so young. It was a unique occurrence in his world. But in Four Claws, it was more than common. It was all of them.

Mother's gaze cut to Father. He dropped his head. "The Raymores' grandmother has the ability to…" He shrugged, looking more defeated than she'd ever seen him. "Every baby goes to her. For her *blessing*."

"And she just randomly assigns mates?" Sylva's incredulous voice rang out through the yard. "That's so *wrong*. How does anyone have that kind of power?"

Father's expression was full of regret. "Speculation is that it's unnatural, but she's ancient."

"Between the power shift and her age, the colony should be safe from now on." Sylva's mind spun. "Just in case, I'll call Jonathon and Demke. They might have more instructions for Harrison and Malcolm."

Mother's mouth was pursed. "We think she somehow passed it on to Shawna."

If so, then the power dynamics were weighted more heavily in the Raymores' favor than she'd originally thought. She should send a direct message to the twins. They might meet more resistance than anticipated. "I need to call Harrison."

"About him." Father's troubled expression wasn't as severe as she was used to. "He's a good guy?"

She wrapped her arms around him. Yes, she was old enough to decide for herself, but knowing Father was watching out for her, that he was determined not to make the same mistake twice, gave her all the love she'd thought she'd been missing.

"Yes," she murmured into his shoulder. "He looks grumpy, and he is, but he's good and I got to choose him."

Father hung on to her for a few more moments. Then Mother came in for a group hug. Sylva squeezed her eyes shut as her chest swelled so full it could burst. Moments like these were what had been taken from her, relaxed and full of love.

Love she had to accept whether she felt worthy or not. If she'd proved herself strong enough and pulled the trigger, would Harrison have claimed her?

Mother pulled back first, dabbing her eyes. "We need to head out. Your father wanted to grab our stuff and get out while those twins are there."

"But we thought it best we not arrive at the same time," Father said solemnly. "Nor was arriving earlier a good idea."

She gave them each a separate hug. "Drive safe. I love you guys."

As she watched them drive off, she dug out her phone. She was about to pull up Harrison's number when her phone rang. Startled, she nearly dropped it. Was it Harrison? Was he calling her as she was calling him?

Smiling to herself, she peeked at the screen. Demke.

Her grin faded as she answered. "Hello?"

"Sylva, thank the sweet mother." He was out of breath, his words rushed. "Get somewhere safe and grab a weapon. John Todd escaped."

CHAPTER 18

*H*arrison was grateful this wasn't some sit-down shindig. After a four-hour drive, the last thing he wanted was to plant his ass in another chair and pretend to be civil.

This meeting wasn't civil. A wizened old grandmother was snarling at them. A young male restrained her on the front porch of her enormous ranch house. Other residents in town had followed them out.

On their way into town, they'd broadcasted—with a bullhorn—who they were and why they were here and to follow them if they wanted to learn the latest news from the Synod and how it'd change their lives.

The convoy of cars had gradually grown until shifters had changed into their wolves and ran alongside instead. Wolves were interspersed throughout the trees surrounding the place, some lounging in plain sight under the early-afternoon sun.

His gaze swept the place. All the homes they'd passed going into Four Claws had been small, plain, and old. Well cared for, but more than a few decades old. The yards were just as plain.

He and Malcolm started a game of "Where do the Raymores live?" as they drove. Any property with a lush, landscaped yard that included more than native materials qualified. As did the homes with more than a couple thousand square feet, like this place.

This sprawling manse sat on eighty acres just outside of town. The house belonged to Grandma Raymore. The male holding her was a distant cousin of Roman Raymore. Half the townspeople were distant cousins of Roman. Most of them were direct descendants of Grandma Raymore.

Roman's family was at the top echelons of power. And he and Malcolm had just wiped out half of them. Except for the sister, but the way this colony treated its females, he wasn't as concerned about her as the brother left alive in the Synod's prison.

Malcolm argued with Grandma Raymore about the Synod's declaration that neither she, nor any of her kin, was in charge. He spoke loud and clear, practically grinning while he verbally sparred with Granny.

Grandma Raymore spat on the ground, her mouth twisted. Harrison studied her. She radiated power. He didn't have to know the history here to understand that no one had ever spoken to her like his twin was doing now. He also didn't have to be clairvoyant to know that the rest of the town, the ones not related to this matriarch, savored the interaction.

"The decision is not yours," Malcolm said. "You can stay here or move, but no matter where you and your pack goes—hell, I don't care if the whole clan leaves—you will no longer hold power over others. All community decisions will be communicated to the Synod through representatives. And we'll pick the reps before we go."

He and Malcolm were constantly monitoring the shifters surrounding them, determining who lacked the strong stench of deceit and rampant, uncaring power. Whose expressions looked like they actually cared about the future of this place? Who didn't look like this was a great opportunity to turn their own pack into the Raymores now that they were out of the way?

His choices were narrowed down to five. Two shifters in the trees, two dudes who had ridden out with them, and the female who was with them.

"The Synod has no say on what we do here." Grandma Raymore's voice rang out, surprisingly strong for a stooped female. "We're an independent colony."

"Are you shifters? Cuz then yeah, they do."

"Dirty fangers have no say over us." Grumbles ran through the audience. A twinkle lit her blue eyes. She'd hit a sticking point, just like they'd known she would.

"Again, that's a yes. The Synod comprises two shifters, a hybrid, and two vampires. But all are in agreement. As are we."

Her jaw worked like she was going to spit again, but she spoke instead. "One of those shifters is a coward who murdered her mate in cold blood and fled the colony."

The crowd went silent. Harrison eyed them. What Sylva had done had rocked them to the point where he doubted few ever mentioned it out loud. The possibility of freedom, of escape. Those who'd fought back like Sylva had probably been dealt with swiftly since then.

Harrison wanted to jump to Sylva's defense, but since her smell was all over him, it was best for her that he kept his mouth shut.

Malcolm would take care of it, and he did. "That shifter is a respected leader on the Synod who bested her opponents. Quite honestly, I'd love nothing more than to see her come down, take you on, kick your ass like she did your grandson's, and *boom!* problem solved. But it's the principle of it all. The Synod said; therefore, you do."

Grandma Raymore smiled and it was eerie. "She'd never win. Shooting a male when he's not looking is not a victory. It's a death sentence, and I'll personally see that she pays for her crime."

"I didn't come here to discuss past transgressions. However, I'd guess your grandsons have a lot worse under their belts. So, it's a moot point." Malcolm swung around and pointed to the two males and the female. "We'd like to have a talk with you."

That was the first time alarm passed through Grandma Raymore's expression. "You don't talk to my people."

Malcolm let out a long-suffering sigh. "We've already covered this. You're not in charge. Shall I repeat the statement?"

Another wad of spit hit the pavement. From the faintly rotten smell she emitted, she must have a bad tooth. A sign of her age, if she wasn't healing from it.

"Why does that male smell like her?"

The yard went quiet again. All eyes were on him. He refused to fidget or twitch.

He met Grandma Raymore's gaze and said in a steady voice, "We've started seeing each other. I didn't have to force her, nor did I want to. It's a new concept. Your family should try it sometime."

If the place had been quiet before, now it was like death had descended. Except for Malcolm's snort next to him.

Grandma Raymore recovered faster than he'd thought she would. "How can we trust you, or the Synod, when you're in her pants?"

"Why should this colony trust a family that has abused its position for centuries?" he countered. Arguing like this was satisfying. He might step in for Malcolm once in a while after this. "You don't have to like it, but your grandsons are gone. They're not coming back. You've already lost and you're the only one who doesn't see it."

Her lips curled and she adopted a knowing gaze. "I'm not throwing in the towel yet."

Malcolm turned his back on her and beckoned the three closest candidates over. "I want to do this in front of everyone."

They approached, but one of the males kept shifting his gaze to the elderly female. Suspicion wafted off him. His gaze would scan the rest of the crowd, then go back to the landing.

"Is something wrong?" Harrison asked.

The male shook his head, then resolution seeped into his gaze. "If the Raymores cause trouble, we have the backing of the Synod? You guys are serious?"

Malcolm nodded. "You'd have priority with the Synod."

The other male looked at his companions. He must've gotten some sort of unspoken approval. "The sister. I don't see her."

"What do you mean?" Harrison asked. He wanted to rub his chest. The need to shift and run full throttle pounded through his veins and hammered at his heart.

"Shawna Raymore. She's been the real power since Roman's death. I don't see her. I think that family is up to something."

"She's not here? At all?" Harrison spun in a circle, glaring at each shifter as he sifted through individual scents.

"No," the guy replied. "I don't think she's even in the colony at the moment."

Harrison lifted his gaze to Grandma Raymore. The glint in her eye was deadly, and her lips curved into an arrogant smile. "Your female is going to pay. She's already lost and she doesn't even know it yet."

～

SSYLVA SLAMMED her front door shut and flipped the lock. Fat bit of good that thing would do. She skidded through the cottage, stumbling over the sudden change in flooring.

She ran down her stairs and found the safe tucked deep into the spare room's closet. Déjà vu, but this time was different. This time she was ready. Flipping the top open, she grabbed the pistol. Light streamed through the windows, making the gun look way more harmless than it was.

It was loaded and ready. She just had to keep from shaking so hard that she accidentally fired. The old-school six-shooter only had five more bullets.

Dragging in air, she willed her pulse to slow down. She could do this. It was her or John Todd and she couldn't lose.

Wishing she'd taken a moment to ask Demke some questions, like how long John Todd had been free, she patted her pocket. Dammit, where had her phone gone?

She'd flung it onto the counter as she'd slid past. Why the hell hadn't she brought it with her?

Was he coming out here alone or were there more? The rest of the Raymores hadn't worried her. The power dynamics meant she'd likely done them a favor. There were now a few siblings closer to attaining control for themselves. But what if they were using John Todd to get to her?

She'd have to get her phone. Jogging upstairs, she tucked the pistol into the back of her jeans.

"Come out, come out, wherever you are."

John Todd.

She twisted her head around, like she could see through the walls to his exact location.

Creeping closer to the front door, she peered out the window next to it. This was too much like before. Except it was a gorgeous August day and her windows were open. Which meant the only thing standing between her and John Todd was a window screen.

Demke was probably sending Guardians out here. But he'd only just called.

Dammit.

"Whore! Turn the gun on yourself yet?" His taunt made her bare her fangs.

"I have a bullet with your name on it," she shouted back. Should she shift? No, then she'd be stuck fighting him until one of them quit moving. She wasn't confident it wouldn't be her.

His laughter was just insulting. "Little Bunny's got some fangs. Too bad they're not earned. This fight is just you and me."

She couldn't let him get to her. Yes, she'd had help in all her previous altercations. And he was correct. It was just her and him. She had no idea when, or if, she'd get any help.

Adjusting her grip on the handle, she kept going until she reached the door. Looking at the wood panel, she willed herself to open it. Cowering in her house was an option, but not one she wanted to pick.

She was done hiding. There would be no more hiding in the pantry. No waiting for the boot to kick her in the gut. No time for someone to get here and fire the gun for her.

Flinging the door open, she hollered, "Do you want to come out, or am I going to have to follow the stink? Who are you with? Anyone I know?"

A deep chuckle came from the direction of her garage. She pounded down the porch stairs, pistol hanging at her side. It'd be like a standoff, but she doubted he was armed.

Did he think his terrible insults were going to scare her off?

He rounded the side of the garage, his slippered feet whispering across the gravel in front of the garage door. She hadn't been lying. She could've closed her eyes and followed her nose.

He stank of sweat. He must've skipped all showers while he'd been incarcerated and she could only guess when last he'd cleaned his ass before driving down to attack her. The stench was overwhelming and she was close to gagging.

At least she'd been mated to the fastidious brother. He'd made her do all the cleaning, but he'd washed himself. That was the only good trait Roman had had.

"John Todd," she said, facing him with her chin up and shoulders back.

"Sylva." His sly smile filled her with oily unease. She couldn't see any weapons. He still wore the prison-issued pale blue jumper. It was grungy and would likely stand on its own, but she couldn't see the impression of any hidden knives or guns. Didn't mean there weren't any.

"How'd you get out?" Would he tell her?

He lifted a shoulder. "I had a little help."

The guards? One of the workers in the building? Anyone could have a grudge against her. Maintenance, the first responders, the jailers. She hadn't made friends, but she didn't think she'd made enemies.

Or had a Raymore blackmailed someone? Threatened their families? She hoped Harrison and Malcolm squashed them.

But she also wished they were here. Harrison's voice would fortify her. His advice could be the difference between life and death.

John Todd didn't prowl closer, only stood there and grinned. She could raise the gun and shoot, but she had shit aim and five bullets. Plus, she wasn't going to shoot a person who was just being creepy.

"Why are you here?" The answer was critical. She hadn't known it until she asked. What *was* he doing here? Why not sneak in and take her off guard?

"Aw, Sylva. We used to be family."

"It was all a lie. I know about Grandma Raymore."

Color drained from his face. "You don't know shit."

"I do. And if I do, you know the rest of the Synod does too." She might as well keep him talking. Maybe he'd reveal a hint of what he was up to. "Harrison and Malcolm went to Four Claws. Raymore Reign is over."

John Todd fisted his hands and his nostrils flared. "You smell like a whore."

"If what I did is considered being a whore, then I'm pretty damn proud of how I smell."

His eye twitched, but he didn't move. Wasn't he going to shift? She'd be less perturbed if he was wandering around naked. Then she'd expect him to shift and try to rip her apart.

The wind ruffled her hair, bringing more of his stench with it. Ugh. That smell.

It was a standoff. What should she do? She couldn't bring herself to open fire. Until he tried killing her, it would be wrong.

Harrison would know. And if he had no ideas, at least she could tell him what Mother had told her about Shawna.

Open your mind. Let Harrison in. He was so far away. Would it even work? He hadn't even claimed her. They might not be emotionally connected enough for mind-speak.

Harrison.

Nothing.

Harrison, I need your help.

She glared at John Todd. He seemed nervous, his gaze glued to her. What the hell should she do?

The hairs along the back of her neck prickled. They weren't alone. She raised the gun to aim it at John Todd and turned.

A smell hit her, a familiar scent, so similar to her mate's. So similar they were related.

Shawna.

A giant wolf stalked around the corner, its teeth bared. Stalking her from downwind and covered in dirt. She would've never smelled the shifter over John Todd. They'd planned this. Would her mental message go through?

She's here.

CHAPTER 19

*H*arrison tried stamping his foot down on the gas, but he'd been driving wide open since leaving Four Claws.

Malcolm had stayed back with the three they'd appointed representatives. If both of them had left, the Raymores would have pounced. Appointing the three non-Raymores was only a start. They'd pick five more—the more the merrier in that type of situation. But Harrison wouldn't be a part of it. He had to get to Sylva.

She wasn't answering her phone. Fucking Demke and Jonathon weren't picking up but had shot him a message saying they'd be in touch. They'd be in touch? That meant shit was hitting the fan in a major way, so major the Synod feared it'd derail what Malcolm and Harrison had gone to Four Claws to do.

A tickling sensation went across his mind. His adrenaline must really be pumping if he kept getting waves of—

No, this was mind-speak. Someone was trying to connect with him. He concentrated on picturing Sylva. It had to be her.

She's here. He was relieved to hear Sylva's voice, but the terror in it made his canines throb.

Shawna had found her. She'd been waiting, watching to see if her brothers would get the job done.

And he was four fucking hours away. *Open yourself to me,* he pleaded. *Let me see what's going on.*

Could she do it? Would she? Was it even possible? Mind-speak was hard enough from this distance, but she was in his head, her voice clear over the roar of the engine.

John Todd's here, too. I don't know what to do.

He managed to keep his internal screaming out of his thoughts to her. How the fuck was John Todd out of prison? That told him why the Synod wasn't picking up. They were too busy communicating with each other and mobilizing new Guardians to find John Todd.

Rage and helplessness coursed through him, but he couldn't let it rob him of his focus. He had contact with her and he wasn't letting go, but mind-speak could be distracting.

Harrison. He could almost feel her shaking.

Picture me seeing what you see, like I'm looking through your eyes.

Would that mean he had to do the same? Would it interfere?

His head filled with a hazy image. It was working!

An advancing wolf with a tawny coat and piercing blue eyes. The world swiveled and there was John Todd, dressed in his prison clothes. The picture morphed with the road he flew down until his was blurry. He was going too fast to be distracted. He'd be no good to her if he crashed into a tree and needed days to recover.

Grinding his teeth together, he let off the gas. His mind still rebelled at not speeding toward Sylva. But she was facing the danger. He'd never get there in time. He pulled to a stop on the side of the narrow road.

His insides twisted at the thought of what Sylva was up against. It'd take more than a few lessons for her to fight both of them, and to do it when one was a shifter and one was a human. *Do you have the gun?*

Yes. Now, she just had to shoot it when she needed to. The picture disappeared. Either their mind-speak wasn't strong enough or they weren't close enough to do both.

No more mind-speak. Just keep me in your head. Nothing. *Come on, Sylva. Let me back in.* Don't keep him hanging during her worst moments. He didn't want to be shut out.

Faint words drifted through his head. Sylva's voice. "I guess this answers the question of how you got out of prison."

The image reformed. John Todd's sinister smile made Harrison's gut twist. He hadn't moved; the *image* was moving. Sylva's house came into view. She was backing away. A swirl and the wolf was back in view.

Ah, she was edging into the clearing to keep either shifter from being at her back. She hadn't been jumped yet, but that just meant that John Todd and Shawna wanted to toy with her.

"Shawna got in and out with no one knowing." John Todd nodded at Shawna, his expression so proud. "I told her everything. How the schedule runs, where the weak points are, and who was shitty at their job."

"I didn't realize you two were so close." The shake in Sylva's normally steady voice was clear. The wolf wasn't advancing, content for now to let Sylva's anxiety spike.

John Todd's sick smile fell. The hostility rolling off him echoed through Sylva into Harrison. "My brother could amplify abilities and that included mind-speak. Until that dog you're fucking killed him."

"Um," Sylva swallowed and her hesitancy to goad John Todd on passed through their connection, "which brother? Because he killed Rafe, not Clayton."

John Todd snarled and stomped forward. His gaze jerked toward his sister. Harrison could imagine the conversation. They were plotting to toy with Sylva until she acted irrationally. She might have piss-poor aim, but she didn't have to be close to peg them with silver.

"We're going to do this slowly, Sylva." John Todd started moving, like he was cutting her off from the trees. "We're going to give you the opportunity to defend yourself. We're going to show you how real shifters get revenge."

The view wavered. *Stay with me*, he urged. *Stay in my head, Sylva. Please.* Never did he think he'd beg another female to access his mind.

The vision sharpened and her voice rang out. "To be honest, I didn't shoot your brother in the back. I pulled the trigger as he laughed at whether or not I could do it."

"Bullshit." The scrunch in John Todd's face resembled his grandmother's. "You and your mama snuck up on him when he wasn't looking."

"He was looking. I was the last thing he saw."

The wolf lunged and the pistol came into view. Good. Nice and steady. But he didn't let that leak into his mind-speak and risk losing the image.

"Stop." Sylva's command was full of Synod authority. "The chance that both of you survive this is slim."

The male's derisive laugh made Harrison want to fly through time and space and punch him. "Nothing a little salt won't take care of." He sucked in a breath and puffed it out. "Enough talk. Time to collect on your pain."

He stalked forward. In the periphery, a blur of tawny fur flew closer. Silver glinted in his view once more. *Do it, Sylva. You gotta do it.*

A growl or a snarl penetrated the din between his ears, but it didn't strike him as wolfish. He couldn't see a damn thing from Sylva's end, and the empty highway taunted him.

He stomped on the gas. Whether or not he made it in time was out of his control, but he had to get to her.

~

HE WAS COMING FOR HER. Murder was in his eyes. *Pull the trigger!*

That wasn't Harrison's voice in her head, it was her own.

Sylva squeezed, barely managing not to slam her eyelids shut. Without bothering to see if she'd hit John Todd, she dove to the side, tensed. Teeth and claws were going to rip into her. A different enraged snarl filled the air. It wasn't her. It didn't sound like a human either.

Rolling to her feet, she clutched the pistol and crouched. John Todd was still coming at her, no visible wounds, but he was cautious, his gaze pinned in the direction of his sister.

Was that...?

Nala! The mountain lion was rolling over the ground with the larger shifter. Sylva would be getting chewed apart if it weren't for the cat.

John Todd dismissed the fight. Shifters were larger than regular wolves and Nala wouldn't last long. He bared his fangs and charged her.

She had four bullets left. Mother's instructions from years ago ran through her head. *Line up the notch.* Closing her left eye, she took aim. *Squeeze.* She hit him. *Squeeze.* It got him in the chest and he staggered, catching himself on the ground with a hand.

Then he straightened.

Breathe, aim, squeeze. She held her breath, looked down the length of the gun to the point between John Todd's eyes, and fired.

His gaze went vacant and he fell to the side midstep.

She was still holding her breath. Wheezing her exhale, she gasped in more air and turned toward the fight. She had one more bullet and she was fully clothed. This shot had to drop Shawna or she was taking on a wolf with her bare hands. And since she was in human form, she couldn't communicate with Nala.

She widened her stance and directed her aim toward the tumble of shifter and cat. As soon as there was an opening, she had to take it. Nala's sides were shredded. Most of the wounds were superficial, but there were enough of them to be detrimental.

Come on, Nala. Get out of the tangle. Give me some distance.

The cat twisted and flipped, evading Shawna's mighty jaws. *Come on, come on.* Shawna flung herself around, dislodging the cat. Nala rolled and flipped up to her feet.

Mother's voice rang through her head. *Breathe. Aim. Squeeze.*

When the gun fired, Nala jumped and spun toward her. Sylva couldn't spare her a glance. Her headshot was success-ful. The wolf staggered, stumbled, then fell to the ground.

Sylva sagged to her knees. Relief poured through her that she was safe. All the siblings that had tormented her were gone.

But she'd killed two beings in just as many minutes. Bile rose in her throat, choking her. Sounds she hadn't heard since Roman had been shot came out of her. Retching, gagging sobs.

Nala limped over to her. The smell of her blood surrounded each of them like a cocoon.

"Aw, hell, Nala. You're hurt again. And because of me." The cat bumped her head against Sylva's shoulder. Sylva dropped the pistol. If she never touched it again, it would be too soon.

Digging her fingers through an undamaged portion of Nala's fur, she murmured, "Thank you."

Sylva!

Harrison was in her head. She wanted to smile—he could break into her head now without permission—but her muscles didn't want to work. *I'm here. They're dead.*

Are you all right? He sounded so worried, so frantic.

Yes. Without Nala, I wouldn't be able to say that. Or be alive.

I'm still hours away.

I'll be here. This was her home. She'd defended it. *Nala's hurt. I'm going to tend to her.*

How bad is she? His concern for the cat bled through their connection.

Her injuries aren't severe, but there are many. So many. Sylva hated that others had been dragged into her drama and hurt, but she couldn't deny that she'd needed help. Wasn't that why they lived in packs in the first place?

Perhaps it was time to open up to the people around her.

Sylva. Harrison was there with her. She liked him in her head. She couldn't expend the mental energy to show him what was going on, but he was there.

Yes?

I... I love you.

She doubted he'd ever said those words. Just like she never had. She suspected he hadn't claimed her because he'd been afraid that he was holding too much of himself back. But then, hadn't she been doing the same? The fear of death changed things.

I love you, too, Harrison. She let him hang out mentally, to know she was okay.

Groaning to her feet, she chatted with Nala. It was the

best she could do to communicate with the cat. "Let me get you cleaned up and find some food."

Nala tried following her, but stopped and began tending to her own wounds. So much blood. The farther she walked away from the cat, the more the air was stained with the sour stench of Raymore blood.

She went into the house, the list of what she'd need running through her mind. Towels. Hot water. Hamburger.

Once she had her armload, she went back outside. Nala was licking at her side. So many injuries, but no bones seemed to be broken and the level of bleeding suggested no major artery had been hit.

Sylva sank down next to her, dabbed a towel in the water, and mimicked the cat, stroking along the cuts. She pushed the meat toward Nala. Pausing, the cat considered the food but went back to cleaning.

"I know it's not Harrison's bone marrow broth, but I'll make some." Manic laughter gurgled out of her chest. "I'll make it whenever you want. I'll make whatever you want whenever you want. Forever."

Nala kept cleaning until an engine broke through the din. The cat jumped to her feet as a plain black sedan flew down the drive. Sylva rose, planning her strategy in case any other Raymores thought they'd come and mess with her.

It was Demke. He was pale, his driving erratic. When he saw her, he hit the brakes, sagging behind the wheel like he'd never been so relieved.

Sylva patted Nala's head. "It's okay. He's a friend." And he really was. She'd never had a friend before. But she could count three now. Nala. Demke. Malcolm. Harrison was so much more.

Nala slunk into the tree line, her wary gaze staying on Demke's car.

Demke clambered out. "Sylva. I thought I was going to be

too late." His gaze landed on Shawna's prone form and his already pale face went ashen. "Malcolm called to inform me — I just— How did you— You know what? I don't care. I'm glad you're still alive." He strode over to John Todd, his lips turning into a deep frown. "Good aim."

She couldn't bring herself to say thanks. She scanned the mess in her yard. Blood and dead bodies. The Raymores' reign of terror was over. She had her life back—and it had been through passive means. "When this mess is settled, how about bringing your family over for a big barbeque?"

"You're worried about him," Sylva murmured. She was draped over Harrison, her head on his chest and her leg across his. The early-morning sun shone through her blinds, hitting the new bedroom set she'd purchased and the flooring that Harrison had installed.

The crook of her neck tingled. He'd marked her again, as he did about once a month.

It'd been six months since he'd moved in, which had been immediately after the final attack. Malcolm still lived at the apartment, but the evening before, he'd announced that he had some loose ends to tie up and would be taking a sabbatical from the Guardians. Harrison translated "loose ends" as something to do with their sister. He'd offered to go, but Malcolm had said he'd plant his ass in an office chair if Harrison tried.

Sylva's smile was bittersweet. She loved seeing how the twins cared for each other every day, and how Malcolm was as fiercely protective over her happiness.

"I am worried about him. We've never been apart."

Harrison trailed his fingers over the mating mark. Tingles spread through her body.

"He'll be fine." She walked her fingers over the hard muscle of his chest. "I'll have to help keep you distracted while he's gone."

"If it's anything like what you did this morning—okay."

She giggled. Every morning was like this. And every day she marveled that this was her life. Before winter had set in, they'd had each Synod member over at one point or another, or all together. She was still pretty isolated, but nothing like before.

Demke's mate, Erin, wanted to learn how to can and preserve. Sylva didn't have her own harvest to work with, but Erin had sent her home with a few jars of whatever they'd worked on. Her pantry stash had a small but solid start. If Harrison would stay out of the applesauce.

Her mind went back to Malcolm's departure. It was the only shadow over their day. Today, they were getting mated at a small ceremony in her cottage. Demke and his family and Jonathon with his were coming out, and Demke would perform the ceremony. Then Malcolm would leave and it'd be harder on Harrison than he'd admit.

"But mostly, I'll use my connections to spy on him," she said.

He chuckled. "Yes, ma'am. But we've been talking." He tapped his forehead. "Up here."

"It's been working?" Pleasure rippled through her. Months ago, she wouldn't want brothers with that close of a connection around her, but this one she actively encouraged.

He nodded. "I won't let him go into full radio silence."

Except that if Malcolm shut him out, Harrison wouldn't be able to stop him. That was a worry for another day. "Everyone's going to show up soon."

"Then we'd better get cleaned up." He rolled up and

yanked her out of bed. She yelped, then laughed as her feet hit the cool hardwood floor.

"Remember when I used to be shy around you and not let you see me naked?"

"I remember it didn't last long."

She laughed and was about to suggest shower sex when movement outside the window caught her eye. "Nala!"

"I'll warm some broth for her."

Grabbing her robe, she swung it around her shoulders and scurried to the door. She stuffed her feet into her thick black boots and shrugged into her parka before going outside. "Nala!"

The cat padded through the snow on silent paws. Sylva detected a change in her scent. She frowned and worked over the change. Nala carried scars from the attack, but overall, she was healthy and as deadly as she'd ever been.

Harrison emerged behind her, wearing nothing but jeans. Even his feet were bare. He set the bowl of broth on the snow. Condensation wafted out of his mouth and from the bowl. "Here kitty, kitty."

The cat ignored him and went to drink.

"Something's off," she said. "Not wrong, but different."

He lifted a brow and studied Nala. "Congrats, mama."

Her mouth fell open. "Cubs! Oh my god, we're going to have mountain lion kittens to spoil?"

Nala hadn't quit coming around, but she only swung close enough for a treat every month or so. She'd moved her den closer to the cottage, and between Sylva and Harrison, they kept other large predators away. And they'd resumed their nightly running routines.

They stood back and watched Nala lap up the broth. Standing next to Harrison, she wasn't affected by the cold. He was like an oven. When Nala was done, she bumped her head against each of them and then loped off.

"Young," Sylva sighed as she went back inside to the warmth of her house. "Can you believe it? It'll be so fun to have them around."

When he didn't respond, she turned as she was shrugging out of her coat. His expression was hard to read, but she detected a mix of fear, curiosity, and hopefulness.

He stuffed his hands into his pockets. "Is that... Is that something you want?"

Having young wasn't something she'd thought about, and it hadn't come up in conversation in the last six months. They'd been fixing up their cottage, entertaining, and talking about when they'd officially bond.

When she'd been mated before, she'd dreaded getting pregnant. The Raymores were one of the most prolific packs she'd ever come across, and her personal nightmare was dutifully birthing and raising a kid that she'd be forced to give away like chattel.

But now? Her life was completely different and under her own control. She thought about what she wanted. "Yes. Eventually." Nerves fluttered in her belly when she asked, "You?"

He mulled it over longer than she'd thought he'd need. "Yes. Eventually. But children terrify me."

"Me, too." She grinned. "So let's worry about getting bonded first."

"My soul is already yours."

His sweet side didn't surprise her anymore, but he could still melt her with his words. "And mine is yours." She held her hand out. "Want me to show you again?"

Desire smoldered in the depths of his eyes. "All the time."

They walked through the house that he'd made back into a home, that both of them had made theirs. Soon, Malcolm and their friends would arrive and she'd mate the love of her life.

It had all started with a dark and stormy night, and she'd made it through to this bright and sunny day.

————

For all the latest news, sneak peeks, quarterly short stories, and free material sign up for my newsletter.

ABOUT THE AUTHOR

Marie Johnston lives in the upper-Midwest with her husband, four kids, and a lot of cats. Deciding to trade in her lab coat for a laptop, she's writing down all the tales she's been making up in her head for years. An avid reader of paranormal romance, these are the stories hanging out and waiting to be told between the demands of work, home, and the endless chauffeuring that comes with children.

www.ingramcontent.com/pod-product-compliance
Lightning Source LLC
Chambersburg PA
CBHW050358190726
48284CB00007BB/2334